Champagne Resolutions

Taya Rune

For information contact :
purplerealmpublishing@gmail.com
ISBN: 978-1-922604-12-5 (ebook)
ISBN :978-1-922604-17-0 (paperback)
First Edition: December 2021

Purple Realm Publishing

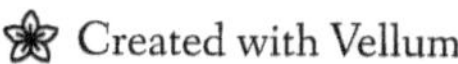 Created with Vellum

Champagne Resolutions

This one is dedicated to every woman.
You are prefect just the way you are.
Xox

"How was your Christmas, Shirl?" Paris asked as she tried not to think about the rolls of skin the seamstress was witnessing as she zipped up the forest green evening gown.

"Quiet, but enjoyable. Most of my family live overseas," the overly tall shop owner answered. Shirl tugged the soft layer of chiffon at the hemline to allow the dress to settle properly over Paris's heavy hips.

The dress was beautiful, with wide shoulder straps made of the same chiffon, but capable of hiding a thick bra strap, as going bra-less was never going to be an option. There was just enough of a deep neckline to draw your eyes away from her thick middle and up to her slightly exposed, ample bosom.

"I am still fat, but the dress is gorgeous," announced Paris.

"Pfft," was all Shirl responded with.

Paris lifted her long auburn hair and twirled it around her head into a quick bun. If she swept her chunky fringe to one side of her heart-shaped face and added a few contouring tricks and some glittering earrings she would almost be okay to look at.

Shirl interrupted her thoughts. "Champagne?" she offered.

"Thank you," said Paris, gratefully taking the glass and having a sip while being careful not to spill it on the stunning dress. "You spoil me."

"Every woman deserves to be spoiled. Whether we are extra tall or extra wide, we all matter." Shirl smiled. The seamstress settled onto the plush bench along the wall that held two other dresses on hooks and coat hangers that Paris had already tried on. "How was your Christmas?"

"Large and loud, fairly standard for a Brendel family gathering. My brothers drive Mum crazy and whinge that they have to give up their rooms to the grandparents and sleep in the barn, when in reality they love being out there, away from the watchful eye of the adults, who are all too familiar with their antics." She took another sip. "I have a shit load of cousins who end up sleeping in the barn if it is raining. It can get quite crowded and there have been many impromptu parties that way. Most of the aunties and uncles bring caravans or camper trailers that go into the closest paddock." Paris had loved returning to the bush for Christmas, but she was happy to be back in the city of Melbourne, where she had chosen to make her career and home.

Paris twirled in her dress and stopped to look at the two others on the wall. One a deep burgundy, the other a soft peach. Both were pretty, but neither made her feel the way the green one did. "I'll take this one. Thankfully there is nothing to alter."

"You always leave it to the last minute. You should try to give yourself a little more time when you are searching for an important dress." Shirl took down the two dresses from their hooks.

"I know. I hear you. I get busy and then the function always rolls around too fast." Paris lied. In truth, Paris always put off buying her dress until the last minute because she was always pretending that this time would be different and she would lose weight before the big event. In the end, she was always frustrated with herself as she hadn't followed through on her plans, and then annoyed that she had left it till the last minute to find a dress. It had become a complicated circle as she spent most of her time completely content with her choices and practicing self-acceptance for her appearance, until an important event cropped up and she had to buy a dress for the occasion, and then she jumped onto the spiral that the world told her she must be thin to find the perfect dress and only then could she find love. Logically, she knew it was rubbish, and subconsciously she struggled with it.

Shirl left the velvet-covered dressing room, carrying the dresses and Paris's now empty glass. It didn't take long for Paris to take off the party dress and hang it carefully before getting dressed and heading out to Shirl to pay for the garment.

Paris loved everything about the boutique and was forever grateful that she had stumbled upon it while looking for a cafe down one of Melbourne's many quirky alleys during her lunch break. It had looked inviting and luxurious and Paris had been drawn to the dress in the window. The dress had been black and red tulle and taffeta, short and low cut. Something she would never wear but secretly longed to —those types of dresses never came in her size. It was a dress you wore to seduce your partner. Paris had stood staring at the dress for several minutes when an exceptionally tall middle-aged woman of average looks had opened the shop door. "It is provocative, isn't it." she had stated.

"It is wonderful," Paris had agreed.

"I am Shirl; I own the place and make all the clothes."

"You have a beautiful shop, Shirl."

"Would you like to come in and try it on?" Shirl had gestured to the black and red dress.

Paris had flushed. "I don't think it would fit me."

Shirl had looked her up and down as if sizing her up. "I think it will fit you perfectly and it will make your partner very happy."

The flush on Paris's cheeks had turned to red heat. "Oh, there is no man."

"Come in and try it on anyway," Shirl had urged.

For some reason, Paris had agreed and found herself in the opulently appointed shop. It had smelled of French perfume, and was covered in rich red velvet, and had an old-world feel to it even though it had the most amazing in-style clothing range. Soft classical music had filled the air and drowned out the city's white noise. Paris still had that black and red dress, hanging in her closet, but she had never found the guy or the courage to wear it.

Paris handed over the forest green chiffon creation and received another glass of champagne in return.

Shirl had a beautiful box all laid out with tissue paper. "A new dress for a new year," she exclaimed as she expertly folded the handmade gown.

Paris smiled. "Now that is something to toast to." She held up her glass to Shirl.

"Got any interesting resolutions for the New Year?" Shirl asked as she wound a huge gold ribbon around the box.

"I don't do resolutions," admitted Paris.

"Oh?"

"Why set yourself up for failure?"

"It can just be a bit of harmless fun. Life doesn't always have to be taken seriously, my young Paris."

"You sound like my mother," she accused.

"A wise woman, your mother." Shirl nodded sagely.

Paris laughed and took a sip of her heavenly champagne. "I promise I will try to have more fun."

"It's not a resolution, but I'll take it," Shirl winked.

The plane made a smooth landing and Xavier Worthington breathed a sigh of relief as the co-pilot welcomed everyone to Melbourne and advised them of the local time and temperature. It was good to be home.

He loved his family, but the pressure he felt to fit in and follow their customs was sometimes overwhelming. Perhaps if Xavier had grown up with it through his teens he would not feel it was so alien, but he had been sent to boarding school, in another country, at thirteen and had never returned to live under their roof. Only for fleeting visits on school holidays did he return, and those were filled with being forced to sit at the dining room table and study. Only the best grades would do.

The airport was busy as he made his way through the International terminal. Summer school holidays had only started a week before Christmas and now that Christmas was done it was time to jet off and explore or relax, and there were always people arriving to uncover the eclectic wonder of Melbourne or returning from their family catch-ups. Xavier found his car easily enough and put on a podcast for the twenty—but could turn into forty—minute drive home. The traffic turned out to be decent and it wasn't long before he was in the elevator traveling up to his floor.

Xavier wrinkled his nose as he opened the door to his small apartment that overlooked the docklands of Melbourne. The place had been closed up for a week and something was giving off a foul stench. "Bugger," he cursed under his breath as he realized he probably hadn't put the trash out before he had flown home for Christmas.

He was excited to be back in the apartment, as he had only recently moved in after having rented it out for the past five years while he was based out of Singapore for work. His family had originally bought the place for him to live in while he studied at University and had given him the property as a graduation gift.

Wasting no time, Xavier tied the rubbish bag together and carried it out and placed it in the garbage chute, grateful that he didn't run into anyone on the way. He couldn't leave the front door open to air out the place and have the neighbors offended, so he opened the glass balcony doors wide and went in search of a sweater to ward off the cool afternoon air. He made a mental note to find a cleaning service to come in once a week, just like he had had in Singapore.

The silence was wonderful after the hectic Christmas celebrations back home in Singapore with his extended family. Xavier had spent a week living with his relatives as he had given up his tiny apartment when he had to take over the rent of the one in Melbourne. Though by most standards in Singapore, the family home was impressive, not uber-rich impressive, but still well above the standard high rise apartments most people lived in. He was not accustomed to sharing his space with anyone, and after a week of his nosey relatives asking personal questions about things he didn't want to discuss he was thrilled to be away from it. He had lived in the boarding section when he had been sent to one of Melbourne's more prestigious high schools, where he had shared a room with another young man, and that was the last time he had shared living space with anyone for more than a few days.

Outside, noises began to intrude; seagulls squawked their never-ending hunger call for food, drivers honked their car horns in frustration of the ongoing chaos of city traffic, and the sound of people laughing and chatting drifted up from the sidewalks where they sat and ate at the restaurants on the ground floor of the apartment block, soaking up their last moments of Sunday afternoon get-togethers before they had to return to work the next day.

Xavier was looking forward to an afternoon of catching up on his emails, watching his favorite streaming service, and maybe starting a new book.

Xavier took the time to unpack his suitcase and put his clothes away properly so he wouldn't have to do it later when he was tired. After taking a hot, relaxing shower where he didn't have to worry about how long he took, as no relatives were wanting to use one of the three bathrooms in the family home, he sent his mother a quick text to say he had arrived safely and to again thank her for a wonderful Christmas when he noticed a new message from his friend, May, reminding him that dinner was at half-past six. Xavier smiled; he was looking forward to seeing his dearest friend and her partner and their beautiful new baby when it occurred to him that he would need to buy the new bundle of joy a gift. And with that thought, all of his ideas of a relaxed afternoon of solitude evaporated.

🥂

The tiny terrier barked aggressively from behind the safety of the lounge room window as Xavier walked up May's gravel driveway. There was no need for them to have a doorbell as Angus alerted everyone in the house regarding any movement outside. The dark stained door swung wide open and there stood his best friend, May, and her wife, Taree, both beaming at him. Taree held their beautiful baby boy, Seb. Xavier gave them both a kiss and handed the gift, a collection of nursery rhymes book over to May. "Congratulations to both of you."

Angus jumped around, demanding his need for attention too, and Xavier obligingly knelt and played with the dog for several moments. "You're a good boy protecting the house, aren't you?" he cooed at the brindle and white scruffy beast. Angus's tail almost wagged off with the effusive praise. And with the welcomes completed, Angus ran off, allowing Xavier into the house.

They chatted as they made their way into the kitchen, where May opened the bottle of wine Xavier had brought, and Xavier took the opportunity to wash his hands after rough-housing with Angus. After toasting to the birth of the gorgeous baby, Xavier could wait no longer. "Okay, hand him over, let me see him."

May laughed. "I win!" She danced around the kitchen.

Taree handed the bundled baby over to Xavier with a grumpy look on her face. "You just couldn't wait until I offered for you to hold him?"

Xavier frowned, a little concerned he had broken some form of baby etiquette. "I didn't know I was supposed to wait until offered."

"Oh, you aren't. I just know how much you love babies and no matter how many times I told Taree she always scoffed. So we made a little wager." May did a little jig.

"Stop the gloating," grunted Taree.

"What was the bet?" Xavier asked, relieved that he had not done anything wrong. He had been raised to always follow proper etiquette and his boarding school experience had enforced it further.

Taree glared at her wife. "May bet that you would ask for a hold within the first five minutes of being here. I said that you would wait until offered because you wouldn't want to offend by being pushy. May very vehemently said that your impeccable manners would be railroaded by your want to hold our baby. That you secretly adore the little bundles of joy."

Xavier looked down at the drowsy, wrinkled face of Seb. He had a full head of straight black hair and gorgeous old man frown lines. "They are completely adorable," he cooed.

"See?" May joked. "Totally smitten."

"What was the wager?"

"Whoever lost has to do all the night feeds for two nights straight."

Xavier winced. No wonder Taree was annoyed. "All I can say is sorry, but your kid is absolutely delightful."

Taree laughed. "Fine, you are forgiven."

The friends spent the next hour catching up and admiring Seb while the roast May had prepared finished cooking in the oven. Xavier only gave up holding Seb when he became fussy and wanted to feed.

As May and Xavier served dinner, Taree breastfed Seb and had him burped, changed, and settled by the time they were ready to eat.

"Impressive," Xavier remarked as she joined them at the table.

"You would think you had been doing that for years rather than just three weeks."

"I am the oldest of six and we are spread out over fifteen years, I have nappy changing down to minimal fuss." Taree winked at him. "Unlike others."

Xavier raised his eyebrows but didn't say anything; he knew May well enough to know she would eventually bite. She did not disappoint.

"So, I am an only child with few maternal instincts, the whole nappy changing and burping I struggle with."

He reached out and squeezed her hand. "I am sure it will become easier," he tried to reassure her.

"I know, I know. It is just a little frustrating when you have a wife that does everything perfectly when it comes to your child, while you struggle."

Taree snorted. "Hardly perfectly. I put his romper suit on backward the other day. Twice," she confessed.

They all laughed at the admission. "That does make me feel a hint better." May smiled fondly at her wife. "So, Xavier, how was the visit home?" She changed the subject.

He shrugged as he chewed on his duck fat roasted potato. May was a chef and had cooked the meal to perfection. "You know. The usual. A loving family, pushy mother, distant father, a house full of aunties, uncles, and their offspring." His heart twisted a little before he said the next sentence. "I am not sure how much longer we will have my grandfather though; he is deteriorating quickly."

"I am sorry to hear that. I know how much he means to you." Both the women reached for his hands to comfort him.

"I tried to spend as much time with him as I could."

They ate in silence for a few minutes.

"Did your mum have any prospects lined up?" Taree asked.

Xavier groaned. "Always. I was expected to meet several suitable young women while I was there."

"And like a good boy you did exactly what your mother wanted?" May smirked.

"You know I did. They were both perfectly acceptable women, who would make fine wives, but..." He let his words trail off.

"Not your type?" May guessed.

"No. Physically petite women are not my thing, you know that."

Taree giggled and winked at him. "No flat-chested women for you, huh?"

Xavier blushed and looked down at his plate. "Taree, stop it," May admonished. "You are making him uncomfortable."

Taree attempted to look sorry, but the glint in her eye told him that she wasn't. "But am I wrong?"

"This lamb is wonderful," Xavier told May, hoping to change the subject.

"Okay, hint taken." Taree cut a piece of meat and held it up. "The lamb is delicious."

May smiled. "Thank you. I am trying out a new marinade."

As they were no longer speaking about Xavier's favored body type, he felt more comfortable owning up to what was truly bothering him. "It's more about the pressure I feel to find the one and marry her immediately. Having a family full of people who met their soul mates early and married quickly puts a lot of pressure on me to settle down. I know she wants the best for me, but at twenty-eight, you would think that she would stop pushing so hard by now."

"Ha!" Taree snorted. "I am married to a woman and have given birth and I am fairly certain my parents still think I am just going through a phase."

May held up her glass. "To parents who mean well, but do not have a clue."

CHAPTER THREE
PARIS

New Year's Eve had arrived. Paris checked her reflection in the compact mirror for the twentieth time to make certain there was no lipstick on her teeth. The forest green chiffon dress floated softly over her curves, and with the killer heels and her hair and make-up done she felt like she could take on the world. Paris was looking forward to spending the evening with her work friends; they were a tight-knit group and she had developed strong connections with several of them. She privately told herself that it didn't matter if no one other than her friends would talk to her or ask her to dance, she would take Shirl's advice and have a good time.

She would be the typical big girl with the big smile and big personality, all the while pretending it was okay for people to ignore her because of her body shape. Paris tried to shake the negative thoughts; her mother would be angry if she knew she was dwelling on them. She had always been told she had been gifted a beautiful name because she was a beautiful girl, inside and out, and anyone worth anything would see that; but her mother had also warned that Paris had to let people in to see it.

"Uber is ten minutes away," Mandi called from the other side of the door. "Let's go, Paris. Everyone else has already left."

Paris checked her teeth one final time before putting the compact away. "You know me, I always like to make an entrance." She opened the office door.

"Wow, you look amazing." Mandi's large eyes were wide with surprise.

"And you, as always, look incredible."

Her closest work friend was five foot four, just like Paris, but where Paris had long, thick auburn hair and hazel eyes, Mandi's platinum blonde hair was cut in a severe bob and she had soft gray eyes. Mandi was lithe and had fabulous muscle tone from years of ballet lessons as she grew up, while Paris was large chested and wide-hipped. They were chalk and cheese. Mandi had grown up in an outer Melbourne suburb, while Paris had been raised in a medium-sized country town three hours out of Melbourne CBD. What they had bonded over, other than a strong work ethic and a want to succeed in their chosen industry, was a wicked and slightly crude sense of humor that made them shriek with laughter at the most inappropriate times.

Mandi grinned. "You are definitely meeting the man of your dreams tonight."

"You do know you say that every time we go out?"

"Well, yes, but this time will be different."

Paris laughed. "You also say that all the time too." They began to make their way to the elevator. "I would love to find the man of my dreams, but seriously, I would settle for a date or a passionate affair with something other than my vibrator."

Mandi gasped with mock horror. "Batteries a little flat?"

"Fuck yeah, it has been quite the dry spell."

Both women collapsed against each other in a fit of giggles. "Sooo..." Mandi drew out the word. "What will your New Year's Resolution be?"

Paris gave her a flat stare. "Very funny."

"Oh, come on, not one teeny tiny resolution?" she needled.

"What would be the point?"

"It's fun?"

Paris exhaled slowly. "Why is it that everyone thinks I am not having enough fun?"

"I know you have fun," Mandi tried to appease her. "I just think people get swept up with the romance of new beginnings and fresh starts. It's like that first kiss, all the build-up of anticipation."

"First kisses sound fun... but no resolutions."

The elevator doors dinging to announce its arrival saved Paris from any further conversation. Mandi's mobile made an R2D2 beeping sound and she looked at it. "Uber is here. David is waiting downstairs with it."

David was Mandi's latest boyfriend and even though she claimed it wasn't love, she spent an awful lot of time talking about him and agonizing over all those things he did as if looking for signs that he cared for her as much as she cared for him rather than just asking. They had met while waiting in line at the cafe next door during their lunch break. David worked two buildings down from their office building and they had been seeing each other for about four months.

The hotel ballroom looked divine, bedecked in a theme of silver and black, with a four-piece band that played a great variety of music that catered to guests of all ages. The large round tables held an impressive selection of party favors in the center, that anyone in the mood could use, from whistles to plastic glittery necklaces, crazy glasses, and hats with the new year's date on them.

Paris's night passed in a blur of laughing with friends and taking her time over the exquisite meal that was served. It was one of those menus where you chose one of two options provided for each course. The first course had consisted of lobster bisque or pork belly with a pureed apple sauce and watercress salad. It was followed by perfectly cooked eye fillet steak with asparagus spears, herbed chat potatoes, and a mixed lettuce salad, accompanied with a creamy bearnaise sauce. The second choice was a flaky pie filled with chicken, leek, and a delectable camembert sauce, that was served with green beans and duck fat roasted potatoes.

The work friends settled around their table as the dessert course was brought out. Paris moaned with anticipated satisfaction as her plate was placed in front of her. Three profiteroles, covered in chocolate ganache, were nestled in a spun butterscotch nest of perfection. A few raspberries were scattered around the plate and Paris guessed they were there to cut the sweetness of the dessert.

Mandi sat next to Paris and moaned with equal wonder as a plate filled with a flawless piece of layered banoffee tart was placed before her.

"To magnificent food, wonderful work colleagues, and a fabulous year ahead." Their boss, Melissa, raised her glass in a toast.

Paris clinked her glass against Mandi's and David's before turning to her right and clinking it with two more work friends. As they settled into demolishing their desserts, David spoke around Mandi. "So, you don't do resolutions, Paris?"

Melissa gave a huge mocking gasp. "No?"

It was well known in the office that Paris thought resolutions were pointless.

David did not know this and was quick to agree with Melissa's shocked gasp. "I know, right? Where is the fun in that?" he turned back to Paris. "Mandi said you don't do them, but not why you don't."

Everyone was watching Paris and instead of being the quiet, shy, school girl who had been bullied and tried to remain in the background, here with her friends she was her true self, someone who was loud, cheeky, and had a dirty mouth.

"How many resolutions have you made over the years that you stuck to?"

She didn't wait for him to answer. "No one makes good resolutions, they are always boring and about deprivation. Fuck that," she exclaimed.

Everyone at the table laughed. They had heard the speech before, some multiple times if they had worked together long enough.

"What do you mean by deprivation?" David pursued the topic.

Mandi laughed, leaned over to kiss him on the cheek, and excused herself. "Good luck with getting her to change her mind." This was the cue for everyone at the table to either head back to the dance floor, finish their desserts, refill their drink, or take up conversations with their seat neighbors.

Paris finished her final profiterole and sighed with delight before answering him. "Have you ever heard a fun resolution? It is always the same thing. I want to lose weight. Be fitter. Go to the gym more. Join a gym. Save money for a car, house, holiday. Stop buying clothes. Clear all my credit card debt."

David held up his hands in what appeared to be surrender. "Okay, okay, I get it. I had never looked at it like that."

"Do you know anyone that has stuck to their resolution after a few months?"

He frowned as he tried to come up with a name. "Can't think of anyone, though I am sure someone has."

"Oh, I am sure someone has but that is the one in the million. I say fuck making yourself feel bad for no reason."

"I can't argue with that." David gave up.

"Good, because I would rather drink and dance instead. The last week has been filled with people telling me that I have to have more fun, so that is what I plan to do for the rest of the evening."

David lifted his glass and nodded his head in agreeance. "I can certainly drink to that."

"What are we drinking to?" asked Mandi as she sat back down in her seat.

"We are drinking to drinking," explained David.

"Well, that is a great idea I can get on board with."

Paris laughed. "Thought you might appreciate it. And we were also drinking to dancing the night away."

"God, another excellent idea. You two are on fire."

David put down his now empty glass and stood. He held out two hands. "Ladies, shall we?"

The women took a hand each and he hauled them out of their seats and dragged them onto the crowded dance floor.

Paris's feet were beginning to ache by the time midnight arrived. The most isolating moment of the entire year had begun. Her friends wished her a Happy New Year before moving on to have a private moment with their partner as the band began a slow song. This was always the time that Paris felt most alone, though she was surrounded by some wonderful people. Feeling like a third wheel, she tried to look at ease as she stepped off the dance floor and moved to hide in the bathroom until the song was over.

"Excuse me." A hand gently touched her wrist.

Paris turned to find a handsome Asian man, dressed in a deep blue suit smiling down at her. From her height, she guessed he was about six foot two inches tall.

"May I please have this dance?" he asked her formally.

YES! her inner voice said while on the outside she hoped she sounded relaxed as she answered. "That would be great."

He took her hand and steered her back to the dance floor. As he pulled Paris into his arms, she noticed Mandi give her a sly wink as she danced intimately with David.

"I'm Xavier."

"Hi, I'm Paris. And no, I haven't been yet," she answered the unasked question.

He smiled and her heart thudded. "I take it you get that question a lot?"

"Yes, though I don't mind."

They danced in silence for the rest of the song. Paris took the chance to notice his strong chin, trim build, and neat haircut. He looked comfortable in what she knew to be an expensive suit, by the feel of it under her hand on his shoulder. This man was beautiful and she responded to his touch immediately. She fought the urge to make the embrace more, for a moment dreaming that she put both hands on his shoulders and then bringing them up to join around the back of his neck as she pushed her body against his. It was a lovely idea to get swept up in.

Eventually, the song ended and she was brought back to reality, which was still pretty hot. Paris stepped away from Xavier. "Thank you for rescuing me."

He frowned at her. "I didn't rescue you. I have been trying to work up the courage for the last hour to come and say hello."

A thrill ran up her spine but before she could answer he held out his hand. A slow smile spread across her face as she took it, and as the band launched into a more energetic song he led her off the dance floor. Without letting go of her hand he walked them over to the bar area, where there were a few empty stools in a quiet corner. At this point, she could feel a current running through their hands and Paris was sure she would have agreed to anything he proposed. He was gorgeous and he made her feel instantly comfortable.

"This is going to sound like I am a stalker or we are

stuck in a bad Rom Com but your smile is wondrous." He leaned forward to be heard over the music and she breathed in his scent. *Holy fuck, this guy is hot.* "It lights up your whole face."

Paris couldn't help it, she laughed. "That is so cheesy."

Xavier joined in her laughter before groaning. "I know, I was cringing on the inside when I said it."

This made her laugh harder. "And have you ever had success with the line?"

Xavier looked at her, his brown eyes serious. "I have never used it before. I am not in the habit of approaching women."

"Is that because you don't need to? Women throw themselves at your feet, I assume."

"Why would you think that?" His handsome face looked confused.

Paris scoffed at his feigned innocence. "Because you are fucking hot."

He raised his eyebrows at her, as if shocked, and then he began to laugh. "Have lunch with me tomorrow. It is the only time I have before I have to fly out for work."

Damn, Paris was disappointed. A wonderful man asks her out and in the same breath tells her he is leaving.

"And then when I'm back on Friday we could catch up on Saturday. That is of course, if I can impress you enough tomorrow at lunch," he continued.

Her heart fluttered. "Don't you think I will need to impress you?" she attempted her first flirtation.

"I'm already impressed. You have a great smile, a kind voice, and some serious dance moves."

Paris blushed deeply. No one had ever said such beautiful things to her. She didn't know quite how to take the compliment. She hoped it wasn't just a line, but for some reason, Xavier just didn't give off that vibe. For one, there was no hint he was drunk; and secondly, he had been a perfect gentleman so far. It felt like there was a connection, but she didn't want to overthink it in case she was misreading him.

"Would you like a drink?" he asked.

"Oh, my drink is on the table. I'll just go grab it." Paris stood at the same time as Xavier stood and their arms brushed. It was the briefest of touches but she felt as if her arm was scorched. "I'll be right back," she managed to choke out as her mind stopped working for a moment and her body was all about the man towering over her.

"I'll meet you back here." He smiled down and Paris's heart flip-flopped.

Paris hurried back to her table and was pounced on by Mandi. "Who the hell is that hot guy?"

"His name is Xavier. He wants to have lunch with me tomorrow..." As she said it a horrible thought came to mind. "Oh, fuck," she swore with gusto.

"What?"

"Well, he asked me out, but I never actually answered him." She clutched Mandi's upper arm. "I am an idiot."

"Don't stand there talking to me, get back there and say yes." Mandi made a shooing motion.

Paris didn't need to be told twice. She refilled her glass and wound her way through the revellers to find where they had been sitting was empty. Xavier had not returned. She looked over to the bar, but he wasn't there either. Had he ditched her? She tried to keep the negative thoughts at bay.

He had appeared so genuine, how had she got it wrong? *Who are you kidding?* Her negative voice intruded upon her thoughts. *Did you really think someone so gorgeous would be interested in someone that looks like you?*

The crowd parted slightly and she spotted Xavier talking to a short, thin Asian woman, dressed in a chef uniform with her straight, shiny black hair tied back. They both looked over at her at the same time and smiled, she waved and sat back down. *See, you panicked over nothing. You are awesome, funny, kind, and smart—much more than just a body,* Paris reminded herself. With her self-esteem firmly back where it should be, she sipped on her drink and waited for Xavier to finish speaking to the woman and return.

"Hi, again," he joked as she stood when he returned.

"I am glad you came back," she said, deciding to be honest and not play games.

"You know you didn't answer my question before? Was it a bit forward? I know most people just start with one date." He leaned in closer and her head spun a little. "Paris, will you have lunch with me tomorrow?"

"Xavier, I would love to have lunch with you tomorrow."

"Okay, but there is one condition."

"And what is that?" She arched an eyebrow at him.

"You have to pick where we eat."

CHAPTER FOUR
XAVIER

Paris was late. Xavier hoped that she wasn't about to stand him up. He checked his phone again to see if she had sent a text—nothing. His heart sank and he was surprised at how much he wanted her to turn up. It wasn't ego either, he genuinely wanted to spend more time with Paris. There had been an instant attraction when he had come out of the kitchen last night to find her smiling and laughing openly with her girlfriend. She had appeared so relaxed and free-spirited; he had been immediately taken with her. Xavier knew he was uptight, his strict, demanding upbringing made him regimented in many ways, he tried to push back against it but it was tough at times. He was also shy when it came to meeting new people, which is why his mother was forever foisting good young women upon him when he returned to Singapore. But they were all very similar to her in appearance and personality, he was certain she wasn't aware of it, and he certainly wasn't going to be the one to point it out. Xavier had spent the hour, while May supervised the cleaning of the kitchen, pretending not to watch Paris enjoy the night with her friends. She was striking in her green floating dress, her auburn hair swept up, and heavy gold bracelet encasing her wrist. He had spent several moments picturing how he would remove the bracelet from her arm and softly kiss her inner wrist, feeling her pulse quicken through his lips. He would be able to breathe in her scent and feel the warmth of her skin. What had spurred him into action, and made him put his shyness aside, was the look of sadness that had appeared on her face when she had begun to walk off the dance floor just after midnight. It was filled with loneliness that had called to his own.

Now he sat in a cute cafe on Ackland Street and hoped that the gorgeous woman he had spent a few hours with last night before her friends had announced they were ready to leave would arrive so he could get to know her better. They had danced several times and had chatted about the basics, but he felt like there was so much more he wanted to know in a hurry. Was this what his parents, grandparents, and great-grandparents had experienced when they had spoken about love at first sight? It was a long family tradition to fall in love and be wed in a short amount of time, but they had all been younger than Xavier was, and he had always assumed that the path was not for him. Like everything, he would try not to conform to tradition.

With a feeling of profound relief, Xavier caught Paris hurrying through the crowd of people strolling along and enjoying the public holiday. Her beautiful heart-shaped face looked upset and flushed as she excused herself while barging through a group of women who had abruptly stopped to chat in the center of the footpath. As she got closer to the table Xavier stood and waved. Her face broke into a relieved smile and she made her way to the small round table.

"Thank God you waited." Paris reached up and kissed him on the cheek before embracing him in a fierce hug. It was unexpected but took his breath away in a way he had not anticipated. She smelled delicious.

"Is everything alright?" he asked; she appeared a little agitated.

"I have had the worst fucking morning." Paris sat in the seat he held out for her. "Thank you."

Xavier was surprised at the swear word. He had noted last night that she had sprinkled her conversation in profanity, and he had assumed it was because she had been drinking and had relaxed, but he was obviously wrong. He didn't typically swear himself and was not surrounded by many people that swore regularly in his everyday life. It was another thing that set Paris apart, though growing up he had noted it was a very Australian thing to swear in everyday conversation.

A waitress hustled over and took their coffee orders and handed them menus. "I love an all-day breakfast menu," commented Paris as she read the specials.

"I have a thing for pastries," admitted Xavier. "Are you ready to order?"

"Oh yes, I am starving."

Xavier beckoned the waitress who came and took Paris's order of scrambled eggs with mushrooms and fried tomatoes and he ordered a ham and cheese croissant.

"A croissant, huh? You weren't kidding about the pastries." Paris smiled.

"It seems I have a thing for all things French sounding." Xavier willed his face not to go red as he attempted to flirt with her.

She laughed loudly, drawing attention from several nearby tables. Xavier loved that she took no notice of the people staring. This was a woman who knew who she was and was comfortable with it. He found it to be a turn-on and was bemused to find that he had to shift position in his chair as his body responded to her loud frankness with appreciation too.

"Your still coming up with those cheesy lines, I see." She reached across the table and squeezed his hand. "Is it wrong for me to admit that I like it?"

Xavier found himself laughing with relief at her comment. "I think cheesy is all I've got, so no, I am thrilled you like it."

She beamed at him before her face changed to a more serious expression. "I am so happy you waited for me." Her eyes were wide and earnest.

Xavier stared at her, lost in those big soft hazel eyes. What he wanted to say was that he thought he had been waiting for her for twenty-eight years, but he didn't want to sound like a stalker or frighten her so he went for chivalrous, "You didn't strike me as the type to stand someone up, so I was becoming concerned about you."

"You are so freakin' sweet." As Paris took something out of her bag the waitress brought their coffees. "This is why I didn't let you know I was running late." She placed a phone on the table in front of him. The screen was shattered.

"That will do it," he agreed. Xavier had put his number

in her phone last night, so he knew that this was something that had just occurred and she wasn't lying.

"I got to the station to find that a train had been canceled and I took out my phone to text you that I would be late when I dropped it and it landed the wrong way." Paris leaned in and lowered her voice. "I cannot tell you how thrilled I was to see you standing here waiting for me."

Xavier took a chance and leaned in toward her, their noses almost touching, if he moved forward a few more inches he would be able to kiss her. The idea was tempting. "You are so beautiful." He stopped talking; those were not the words he had been meaning to say. It seemed his mind was going in a different direction than he had intended.

Paris moved a fraction closer and tilted her head slightly. "You are gorgeous," she whispered, her breath hot and inviting.

Before he could talk himself out of it he moved those last few inches and kissed her. Softly, sweetly, with a hint of pressure and a promise of what could be more.

CHAPTER FIVE
PARIS

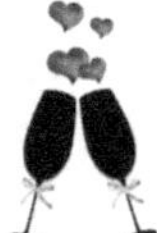

"*Mum*, how are you?" Paris answered the phone and put it on the loud speaker as she continued to make her bed.

"All is well. I was just calling to check-in, you haven't rung this week." Her mother's strong country twang filled the air.

"Yeah, sorry. I have been flat out at work. So many people take holidays around this time, and the rest of us have to pick up the slack."

"Paris, don't you let them work you too hard." Kathleen was always quick to tell Paris that she was being taken advantage of, even when she wasn't. Kathleen would have preferred Paris to stay in the town she grew up in and work for a local business rather than move to Melbourne and work for a large company that matches universities with overseas students that wish to study abroad. Paris found the role rewarding in so many ways; there was nothing like finding the perfect fit for the student.

"They don't work me too hard, Mum. I love it. It is just

a busier time of year as we focus on putting so many things in place at the beginning of a new school year." Paris put the final pillows on the bed and drew the curtains open to reveal a gorgeous summer day. The forecast said it was going to be a scorcher. "How's Dad?" She changed the subject.

"Just like you, working too hard."

"Isn't Kent able to help out more?" Paris's youngest brother, Kent, was a third-year apprentice in the family mechanics business.

"He does as much as he can, you know what your father is like."

Paris's phone beeped and she snatched it up, impatient to see who had messaged her. Xavier had flown back in last night and had promised to text her this morning with plans for the day. This would be their fourth date over the past ten days and it was his turn to choose what they would do. Paris stared at the screen as her mother's voice filled the bedroom. Paris's excitement had swiftly turned to dread as she reread the text.

Bring a swimsuit, towel, and something to tie your hair back with. I will be there to pick you up in 30 minutes. Xavier. Xxx

She was so focused on the swimsuit that she almost missed that he had finished the text with kisses.

"Paris, are you listening?"

"Shit, sorry, Mum, I just got a message that surprised me."

"Is everything okay?"

"Yes, all good. I think I am heading to the beach with a friend."

"Sounds likes fun. I will let you go to get ready."

Paris loved that her mum was so easy going about things. A few of Paris's friends had parents who were demanding on their time and that their child always had to be the one to make contact. Kathleen would have preferred Paris to live a little closer but was thrilled that her daughter had followed her dreams and was living her best life.

"Thanks, Mum. Talk soon. Love you."

"Love you too, Honey."

Paris checked that her mum had hung up properly before she began to swear heavily. Kathleen didn't mind a little casual cursing, but the colorful language that filled Paris's bedroom would have earned her a talking to regarding ladylike behavior.

Paris sent an answering text and decided to respond with the same amount of kisses.

I'll be ready. xxx

It took her a few minutes to locate her swimsuit as they were shoved in the back of a drawer. She found the sarong that Mandi had bought for her the last time she had holidayed in Bali and then went in search of her beach towel. Paris found the towel handily placed beside her large woven straw bag in the linen cupboard with an old tube of sunscreen and a slightly deformed sun hat in the bottom of the bag. Trying not to think too much about it, she grabbed the bathing suit and went into the bathroom to have a quick shower.

Within another ten minutes, she had her bathers on and

the sarong wrapped around her waist with a cute matching colored t-shirt, with a plunging V neckline. Sunglasses currently held her auburn hair from her face, but she had an elastic around her wrist to hold her hair back as instructed. A pair of cute flip-flops with glitter finished off the ensemble. Paris thought she looked great, she just didn't want to think about the swimsuit underneath.

Before she could second-guess herself and go and change into another suit her doorbell rang and her heart beat a little quicker. Xavier had arrived.

The first ten days of January had been bliss. Xavier was a pilot for Singapore Airlines and was currently assigned the Melbourne to Singapore run. Paris found the whole thing romantic as he flew in and they spent their time together. They took it in turns to think of places to go and things to do, which Paris adored.

Paris opened the door to reveal the tall, handsome man who she suspected had already stolen her heart, but she wasn't prepared to think about that yet. She kept trying to tell herself that it was too soon. It only happened in movies. And that she was confused because the men she had had anything to do with only wanted to sleep with her and move on because she was just another warm body.

"Hi," she greeted him with a kiss that quickly turned into a passionate embrace. His lips were firm against hers. Paris pushed her body hard against his in response to his soft moan and she could feel him harden against her. It was a satisfying moment to know she had such an effect on this incredibly handsome man. Xavier had shown himself to be quite self-contained and this moment of passion was intoxicating.

Xavier took hold of her hips in his hands and slowly pushed her away, breaking their kiss. "Hi," he breathed and rested his forehead on hers. "I missed you," he spoke the words so softly she almost didn't hear him.

"I missed you more," she whispered as if it were a secret. Paris wound her hand in his thick dark hair and pulled his face towards hers to kiss him again. She loved doing that.

With regret, Paris let go of his hair and broke off the kiss. "If we don't leave now I might not remain a lady and instead invite you in to spend the day in bed." She gave him a cheeky grin to show she was joking, but at the back of her mind, she was silently pleading for him to take her up on the offer.

As always, his gentlemanly ways showed themselves and he took a step back from her. Paris's groin protested in response. She turned and locked the door before grabbing her straw bag and following him to his car. The BMW was a convertible and he had put the roof down. Paris understood the need to tie her hair back now. Xavier held out his hand and Paris went to take it when he shook his head. "No, give me your bag, I'll pop it in the boot."

"Thanks." She handed him the bag, which he slung over his shoulder. Then to her bemusement, he held out his other hand to her.

Xavier

Xavier watched Paris from behind his sunglasses. She was slowly letting the fine yellow sand trickle through her fingers and fall onto an ever-growing pile. She had been unusually quiet since they had arrived at the beach over an hour ago. They had laughed and she had sung—badly and loudly—to the radio on the trip down the freeway to the peninsula, but as soon as they had settled onto their towels and he had removed his shoes and had laid back to soak up a few rays of sun he had felt her nervousness. Had he miscalculated bringing her to the beach? She had said she liked water and swimming.

As it was the summer holidays the beach was busy with families, teenagers out with their friends, and couples holding hands and walking along the shoreline. Tennis balls whizzed by occasionally as beach cricket, a great Australian pastime, was played close to the water where no one ever placed their towels in case that one freak wave came that was a little too high and soaked everything. Xavier had always loved the atmosphere. Laughter, music from portable radios, and children squealing as waves chased them filled the air. But today all he could focus on was the wonderful woman beside him as she watched the waves and struggled to make conversation.

"Paris, is something wrong?" He spoke softly as people were surrounding them and he didn't want them hearing their conversation.

"No nothing," she replied too brightly to make it believable.

He held up the sunscreen bottle. "If you take off your top I would happily rub some sunscreen on your shoulders and back for you," he offered. The thought of touching her bare skin was enticing.

"I am not sure I am going to swim yet."

"I thought you liked to swim?"

Paris looked over her shoulder at him. "I did say that, didn't I?"

He sat up slightly, resting on his elbows. "Yes. You said you like to swim in the slow-running river at the back of your parents' property. That's why I thought the beach would be a good idea."

She looked around before looking back at him. "I am not used to so many people."

Xavier was finally beginning to understand what the problem might be. He sat up and lifted his sunglasses so she could see him. "We can leave if you like?"

She shook her head. "No, it was your date choice and you wanted to bring me here. It was a wonderful and thoughtful thing. I am being silly."

Gathering all of his nervous courage as he had never wanted anything to be as perfect as the time he spent with Paris he crawled over to her towel and sat behind her. "Please just take off the t-shirt."

She watched him for a few moments more and he held up the sunscreen and waved it at her, a hopeful smile on his face. "Okay."

Paris turned back to face the water and slowly pulled her top over her head, exposing beautiful soft shoulders and a navy blue swimsuit with a crisscrossed back. As he slowly rubbed the white lotion on her shoulders he noted the cute freckles that ran along the tops of her shoulders, they were the same color as the ones that were on her cheeks and nose.

What Xavier wanted to do more than anything at that moment was slowly draw the strap off her shoulder and kiss her exposed neck. He pulled his thoughts away from that idea to keep his body from betraying his lustful notions. What he did instead was move to whisper in her ear, "Your skin is so smooth, it's perfect."

Paris shivered slightly in response but said nothing.

Xavier eventually completed applying the lotion, but instead of moving he spread his legs out on either side of Paris and drew her back to lean against his chest. He felt her hesitate for a moment before allowing him to move her. As she settled against him she looked up at him with a small smile, he couldn't help but notice that she had placed her hands over her stomach. He wanted to make her laugh, to dissolve the tension she was displaying. "I think I definitely have the best view now." He winked down at her, which was something he never normally did. He found it empowering, especially when he saw her eyes widen and her breathing change.

It took her a few moments and her moving her own head to look down to realize that he was staring at her cleavage, which was ample and exposed to him from higher and behind her. "Now, that wasn't cheesy. That was just plain naughty."

Emboldened by her answer, he kissed her on the top of her head. "Do you prefer cheesy or naughty?"

"From you, I will take either." Paris looked up and winked back at him.

He could feel her relax slightly, but she wasn't back to her normal self that he had come to find so attractive so quickly. They sat there for a quarter of an hour watching the world go by and the gentle waves roll onto the pristine sand. Xavier was getting hot; it was time for a swim. He just hoped he could get Paris to join him.

"I am going to go for a swim. Are you coming?" He hoped his voice was light and casual.

Paris sat forward to allow him to stand. Once he was standing he held out his hand to her to help her up. "Paris?"

She looked at his hand and up at him as if considering something. "It is hot today," she conceded. Slowly she took his hand and he pulled her up. They stood there looking at each other for several moments until he realized there was something he could do to help her realize that he understood more than what she thought he did about body image and people's judgment.

Without hesitation, Xavier took his swim shirt off, smiled at her, and waited.

Paris

*P*aris bit her lip in an attempt to not say something completely inappropriate. She had figured that Xavier was toned underneath his clothes as when he held her his body was hard and strong. She hadn't counted on the Adonis-like torso with the washboard abs. *Fuck me*, she said quietly in her head. She put her hands behind her back in an effort to not reach out and run her hands over his pecs, after all, they were in a public place. "You going to put sunscreen on?" she asked.

"You want to help me?" he grinned.

"Absolutely." She moved to retrieve the bottle and as she straightened she saw a young boy pointing at them before his mother hastily turned him around and knelt to talk to him. Paris frowned; that was a little odd. It was then that she noticed several others look at them and quickly look away as she looked in their direction. She dismissed the odd behavior and held up the bottle. "Turn around."

Paris waited with anticipation as Xavier slowly turned, she loved a man with strong back muscles and if his front was anything to go by his back was going to be magnificent. She was right, his back rippled with corded muscle and Paris wondered where he found the time to go to the gym. He finished turning and Paris drew in her breath as she took in the large port wine birth mark that covered a third of his glorious back. It ran from the bottom of his left shoulder blade toward the center of his back and traveled down his spine, crossing over to the right-hand side and thinning out as it disappeared into the top of his shorts. Now she understood the rude stares and the mother's rush to talk to her pointing son. "Fuck," she swore under her breath, but it was loud enough for Xavier to hear her.

He looked over his shoulder. "What?"

She placed her hand in the center of his back and almost melted under the feel of the bunched-up muscles, she realized he was exposed and anxious. "I am a sucker for a beautiful back and yours is fucking incredible. How long do you spend in the gym and can I come to watch you work out?"

He laughed the loudest she had ever heard him laugh and his muscles relaxed underneath her hand. As she began to apply sunscreen he began to talk. "I usually keep my rash vest on while at the beach because the sand can sometimes irritate it, but I do need a bit of sun on the chest now and then."

As her hand moved over the birthmark she was surprised to find it felt the same as the rest of his soft skin. "Does it hurt you at all?"

"No, it can just be a bit more sensitive."

"So, you only took it off to get a bit of sun?"

"Have you finished?"

While she wanted to stand there and rub cream into his back for the remainder of the day, she didn't want to chance it and irritate his skin. "All done."

Xavier turned around and kissed her on the nose. "Thanks." He looked at her, his gaze serious. Paris longed to get lost in his brown eyes. "I took my shirt off to get a bit of sun, but to also show you that it doesn't matter what other people think of you. I have lived my life with people staring and pointing and it used to bother me, but now I just don't care. I learned that accepting myself was far more important than having others' acceptance." This time he kissed her firmly on the lips before pulling away. "Be you, Paris."

She softened with his words, her insides tightening at his close proximity and heated kiss. Paris was surprised at how strongly she cared for this man. "I do try. I think most of me is pretty great."

"I think all of you is dazzling in every way. Can you please take off that sarong, so we can go swimming? I am frying here."

Paris took hold of her insecurities and shoved them aside. This man had exposed his vulnerabilities to make her feel comfortable, and he told her often how wonderful he thought she was and looked. Paris wanted to believe he was being truthful, but she struggled to trust people as her best friend, Tracey, had turned on her when she had started dating the high school playboy. The pair of them had made Paris's life miserable for two years until Paris had left to go to University in Melbourne. *Xavier is neither Tracey nor Jack. He has been respectful, wonderful, and has shown you he desires you in so many ways. Shirl and your mother both want you to have more fun, so let's go have more fun.* The voice in her head was almost shouting to get her point across.

With shaking hands, because in all honesty, she had built this up to be far more than it was, Paris undid the knot in her sarong and let it slip down to her feet. The world did not end, people did not gasp with shock, everyone continued to enjoy their Saturday afternoon, and Xavier beamed at her. Her fears fell away and she grinned back. "The first one in the water gets to pick where we eat tonight." And with the challenge issued, Paris dashed towards the water.

CHAPTER SIX
PARIS

"Oh my God! What is that horrid smell?" Paris stood at the door of Xavier's apartment.

The gorgeous man looked mortified. "It looks like I forgot the rubbish again. I keep meaning to organize a cleaner. I got in later than I thought I would last night and didn't notice it then. This morning, I was in such a rush to pick you up that I wasn't paying attention."

Paris laughed. "Well, it is good to know that you aren't perfect."

Xavier grinned. "If you want to wait here I will be brave and go and retrieve the offending trash."

"Ah, my knight in shining armor."

"Or you can hustle that beautiful bottom of yours out onto my balcony and take in the water views while I get rid of the smell. Your choice?"

Paris wasn't paying attention, her brain had stopped working when he had mentioned her arse.

"Paris?"

"Shit, sorry. Zoned out for a minute. The balcony

sounds grand."

She followed him into the stinky apartment and wrinkled her nose as she tried to ignore the smell. Once they were out in the open air on the balcony she took in a deep breath as if she had been holding her breath. Xavier flushed with embarrassment, which made Paris feel bad for her antics. "I will be right back. Would you like a glass of wine?"

"Yes, please."

"White or red?"

"Don't care. Surprise me." Paris watched Xavier walk through the spacious living area of his apartment, all furnished in chrome, black and red, it was a lot sexier than what she thought he would have. The couches were over stuffed and only one faced the television, while the other had a perfect view of the bay. She raised her eyebrows as he bent to retrieve the offending garbage bag, his arse was spectacular in his board shorts.

"Enjoying the view?" he spoke as he stood and she had the grace to blush.

"It's very impressive."

Oblivious to what she had been admiring he walked through the lounge, holding the bag out at arm's length. "I like to sit on the couch on rainy nights and watch it come down. It's even better when we have summer storms and I can open the doors to let that fresh rain smell in too."

"Sounds wonderful," she agreed as she turned to admire the view he was talking about.

It didn't take long for him to return, wash his hands, and pour them a drink.

"So, what do you think?" he asked as he handed her a

glass of white wine and joined her on the balcony.

Paris took a deep breath and decided to go with flirty rather than safe. After their discussion on the beach about acceptance in all forms, she wanted to be true to herself and not worry so much about impressing him. From all appearances, it seemed he was already impressed. "I think we should discuss your feelings about my butt?"

Xavier smiled and his brown eyes twinkled as he looked down at her. "It is gorgeous," he said softly as he stepped closer to her. He reached out and pushed her long fringe out of her eyes. "I also love your curvy hips and from what I could see in the cute bathing suit, you have breasts that I long to bury myself in."

A tingle crept along her spine. Paris had had men talk dirty to her and compliment her on occasion to get her in bed, but never like this. Xavier's clean dirty talk was enticing. "Kiss me," she whispered.

Xavier took the wine glass from her and placed both his and hers on the glass table beside them. His handsome face filled with care, smiled at her as he lowered his head and their lips connected, soft and gentle. She moved her hand up and entwined her fingers in his dark hair while she snaked the other one around his back and found her way under his shirt.

Xavier's kiss became more urgent and his tongue sought hers. He brought both hands up and cupped her jaw, his fingertips resting in her hair. He stopped the kiss and pulled back from her slightly, his eyes serious. "I want to make love to you. I want to worship every inch of you."

Paris's soft smile turned into a wide grin.

"I did it again, didn't I?" he groaned.

"It may have been a tad cheesy," she admitted. "Though I like the sentiment, I am covered in sand."

His face filled with confusion for a moment, before clearing. Paris wondered what he was thinking. "That's fine. I am not going anywhere, perhaps another time." Xavier put his finger under her chin and drew her face up to his. "I am happy to wait. We can always make out on the couch?"

"No, you misunderstood me." She pulled his lips back down to hers and kissed him as passionately as she knew how. When they broke apart they were both breathing heavily. "I wanted to borrow your shower..." She let the idea hang there.

Understanding dawned across his square face and he smiled. "I'll get you a towel." Xavier held out his hand. "Come."

Paris took his hand and followed him down a hallway and into a stark white bathroom, where lush red towels hung from chrome towel racks. "Feel free to use anything in here. The towels are fresh."

"Thank you."

He kissed her cheek and firmly closed the door behind him. Paris decided to get undressed in the shower cubicle as she didn't want to get sand on the sparkling white floor tiles. She took off her t-shirt and sarong, giving them each a good shake before folding them and placing them on the side of the tub. Checking that the shower had soap, shampoo, and conditioner, Paris turned on the water and even though it was a hot humid night, still had the water temperature on hot. She rinsed out her bathers once she had removed them and hung them over the top of the shower screen.

Paris focused on the warm water and cleaning her hair and body of the salt water and sand that she had brought home on her. Her mind wandered to the picture of Xavier and his perfect chest hovering over her and she felt an equal measure of anxiety and longing.

This would not be her first time, but in many ways it felt like it was as this was the first time it wasn't a one-night stand where a man was whispering anything he thought might work to get her to do what he wanted. Paris had been happy with that at the time, as her desires for contact and wanting to be wanted were strong enough for her not to care about an emotional connection. She knew tonight would be different. There had been a connection between her and Xavier from the moment he had held her arm to stop her from moving off the dance floor.

It was only after she had dried herself and wrapped her hair in a towel did she consider what she was going to wear out of the bathroom. Was just a towel too forward? Should she perhaps put the sarong back on, tying it above her breasts?

There was a polite tap on the door. "Paris, did you want to borrow a t-shirt or something?" Xavier asked.

She laughed and her worries melted away. "I was just considering what I might wear. What are you wearing?"

"Currently just a towel. I had a shower too."

The answer made up her mind for her. "Don't move," she said through the door. Paris took the towel off her head and shook out her hair so it hung in damp waves and her heavy fringe she gave a quick finger comb. Satisfied that her hair was decent, she took a deep breath and opened the door. Her core lit on fire as she discovered Xavier leaning patiently on the opposite wall. His hair was spikier than normal and his arms were crossed over his chest, showing off his defined triceps and biceps. Paris's breath grew shallow as her desire rose as she took in the towel wrapped low around his hips, showing off the tiny line of fine hair that trailed from his navel down into his towel. With a sense of lustful abandon, she boldly moved toward him and pushed him up against the wall, her hands on his pecs. His chest was smooth, his nipples became firmer as she pinched them with her fingertips. She kissed him deeply, her tongue searching for his before trailing kisses along his jawline to his earlobe and then licking upwards while breathing where her tongue had been. She felt Xavier shiver under her hands.

Thrilled with his response, Paris grew more adventurous and began to kiss and lick back down his throat and onto his chest. His hands came to rest on her shoulders and he squeezed them tight as she took one of his nipples into her mouth and sucked gently before nipping it with her teeth. His hips pushed against hers and she felt his erection, strong and hard against her stomach. Grazing her nails down his chest and over his rock-hard abs she traced the line of soft hair that ran from his navel down into his towel. Her mouth followed, nipping and sucking as she went. Xavier softly spoke her name and fisted her damp auburn hair. She felt no downward pressure from the hand still resting on her shoulder and knew that the next move was hers to make, with no pressure from him. He was still a gentleman and it made her wet to think about trying to break through his well-behaved exterior to the horny, free-spirit beneath.

Paris ran her fingers along the edge of his towel before

tugging at it and allowing it to fall to the ground. His erection was free and it was amazing. He was thick and hard and a bead of precum sat on its tip, inviting her to do with it what she wished, and what she wanted was to devour him.

Xavier made to move, taking his hand from her shoulder and putting it under her arm as if to bring her to a standing position. She grinned against his lower abs and refused to budge, instead dropping to her knees and pushing him back against the wall with her hands on his lower hips. She held the base of his cock and brought her tongue to the tip, swirling it around the crown and licking along the thick vein underneath. He was delicious and she looked up to find him watching her, his hooded brown eyes half-closed and mesmerized. "You are magnificent," he told her.

She responded by taking him into her mouth, sucking and licking as she went. She pulled the skin-tight at the base of his hard-on and with triumphant glee felt his fist tighten in her hair as he began to slowly take control and fuck her mouth. She moaned and he shivered in response, his cock was so thick that she stretched her mouth further than she had ever needed to before, and all she could think about was how amazing it was going to feel to have him inside her. Her core tightened, making her groan against him. If she kept this up she might not need him at all to make her orgasm, the thought of him alone might be enough.

Suddenly he stilled and Paris gently kept the pressure around his cock with her hand. "Paris, stop." His breathing was labored. "Please."

"Only because you are so fucking polite." She looked up at him grinning wickedly. She allowed him to help her get back to her feet.

He leaned over and kissed her before nibbling on her earlobe, sending a chill down her spine. "Come with me to the bedroom and we shall see just how polite I really am," he spoke quietly in her ear.

"Lead the way." She stood aside.

Xavier retrieved his towel from the floor but didn't bother to wrap it around his waist. Paris's breathing hitched a little as he walked in front of her and she noted the large birthmark stopped about midpoint on his tight arse cheek. His back muscles rippled and her tummy butterflies swirled as she became suddenly aware that she was about to be naked in front of this chiseled god. Her bravado faltered. *Shit,* she thought to herself. She stopped in the middle of the hallway.

Xavier looked over his shoulder to find her standing still. "Paris?" His voice was filled with concern. He wrapped the towel around his waist, but it did nothing to hide his hard-on. She would have giggled if she was in a different head space. He moved slowly back to her like she was a scared, timid animal. He took her chin with his thumb and forefinger and raised her face to his, ever so gently he kissed her. "I want this. I want you. Your soft curves are all I think about."

Paris's heart swooned at the words and her butterflies settled and transformed back into flames of desire. "Can we turn the lights out?" she whispered, looking up through her lashes she tried to appear coy rather than anxious.

"I want to see you, but I understand." He kissed her again, sliding his tongue along her bottom lip.

She sighed and breathed into his mouth. "You can leave the curtain open and let in the moonlight." Paris lifted her arms and placed her hands around his neck as he deepened the kiss.

He slowly walked her backward into the bedroom, flicking off the switch as they went past. "Lay on the bed, face down, you can leave the towel on." He spoke firmly and her insides heated further. This was a side she hadn't experienced before, and she hoped to see more.

Paris did what she was told. Turning her head as she laid down to watch him push the heavy curtains open, allowing the weak crescent moon's light to filter through the tinted windows. She kept her towel on but had loosened it. He turned and looked at her. "Is that okay?"

"Yes."

She watched his shadow move toward the bed, it wasn't until he took it from the bedside table did she notice a bottle. The room was dark enough that everything was in silhouette. He knelt beside her and poured a little of the cold liquid on her upper back, and she wiggled as her skin tingled. The smell of sweet strawberries filled the air.

"Relax," he spoke softly in her ear before nipping it. Without out warning, he straddled her upper legs and she smiled to herself as his cock nestled on her arse—he was still hard.

Slowly he rubbed the oil across her shoulders, lifting her hair and pooling it to one side so he could reach her neck. With strong hands, he massaged her shoulders and neck before moving her towel halfway down her back and kneading the muscles in a circular motion. It was heaven. Inch by inch he moved the towel down until only her bottom was covered, and Paris was enjoying the massage so thoroughly that she barely noticed. Xavier shifted his weight and began to move down the bed, drawing his hands over the back of her thighs and down her calves. She felt the bed move and he held her ankles, gently pulling them apart a fraction at a time, she put up no resistance. Xavier knelt between her now open legs and scraped his nails back up, making her shiver as he glided over her inner thighs and up under the towel. He tugged on the towel and she rolled her hips from side to side enough for him to pull it free. Xavier tossed her towel to the floor and then she watched his towel fall too. Paris closed her eyes and focused on the sensation of his hands caressing her arse. "I told you it was beautiful," he announced as he bent down and kissed it. Sucking and biting as his hands ran up either side of her spine and back down. He ran a hand over the crevice between her cheeks, she jerked slightly at the odd but pleasant sensation as he moved over her butt hole, which no one had ever touched before. He continued down and she lifted her hips slightly, allowing him access to her core and essentially giving him permission to do what he will.

"Oh, Xavier," she breathed as she moved her head and buried her face in the pillow.

He pushed one finger inside her and she clutched the sheet, trying to savior the feeling while anticipating what he would do next. Xavier put a second finger inside her and Paris exhaled heavily as his in and out movements became stronger. She lifted her hips higher still and he circled his thumb around her anus making her bite her lip. *Farrrrk*, he was amazing. Xavier trailed kisses up her back as he took his fingers from her. She vaguely felt his arm moving and wondered what he was doing. Was he reaching for something? It dawned on her. "You don't need one. If you trust me that is, as I trust you."

He didn't answer, he simply stopped his search for a condom she assumed he had placed somewhere earlier. Both his hands returned to her body and he pressed his torso against her back, bringing his cock closer to her core. He rocked back and forth, rubbing the head over her clit and she grunted with pleasure. Her slick wet folds making him wet enough that when he moved a fraction further he slowly sank into her an inch at a time. This time his moan joined hers.

Paris lifted her hips, pushing back until she was up on her hands and knees. He buried himself fully in her again and again, the only sound filling the room was their heavy panting. With impressive self-control he slowed his motions as he brought a hand around to grasp her full breast, tugging and pinching the nipple. Her want grew, her core tightening as he rolled the nipple between his fingers before letting go and moving down her stomach to her clit. Xavier stroked her as he increased the intensity of his thrusting, Paris knew she was about to tip over, she couldn't hold on any longer. Her body shook with the first wave of her orgasm and she dropped to her elbows, resting her forehead on the bed as he continued to pound into her. Her muscles clenched over and over, which sent him spiraling into his own shuddering orgasm. He collapsed on her back, kissing her neck and reaching up to rest his hand on her breast. Paris wanted to say something but she was struggling to catch her breath. She wondered how long it would be until he was ready to do that again.

CHAPTER SEVEN
XAVIER

It was only when the sun began to peak through the window did Xavier realize he hadn't closed the curtains after the second time they had sex. It was a false dawn, so they still had plenty of time before the room got too hot if he didn't get up and close it. He knew he should close it to make Paris feel comfortable when she got out of bed, but he was warm, and content, and the idea of moving his arm that draped over Paris and loosely held her rounded stomach was unappealing. He wrestled with what he should do as he relived the memories of last night. His cock twitched in response to his thoughts.

She was gorgeous, sweet, kind, and smart. He liked that she laughed easily and didn't take things too seriously. He knew he tended to overthink so she was quick to draw him away from that with her quick banter and hot kisses. She swore a little too much for his liking, but he had to admit her dirty mouth last night had been a turn-on—though he knew he could never have said what she did. The only flaw he could see was her insecurities with her body. He did have some understanding of what it was like to not be happy with your body, but when he came to terms with the fact that most people had something about their appearance that they didn't like it made it easier for him to deal with his feelings about the huge birthmark on his back. It was only when he had hit his teens and he had started to take his shirt off, wanting to impress the young girls with his naturally sculpted physique did he experience negative reactions. Once most people got over the size of it they stopped staring, but a few of his peers had been cruel in their jibes and comments. This had continued when he moved to Australia for schooling. Most people just stared, only small children commented, or those with truly no understanding of propriety, and once he had understood that most were more curious than repulsed did he come to the conclusion that he simply needed to accept all of himself and ignore any hurtful stares or comments. It had been a freeing moment.

Paris was going to have to find that peace one day too. Society was so caught up in being told what was acceptable and sexy that it forgot we are also varied and flawed. Waif-like women did not appeal to him, the media's ideal standard did not appeal to him. He adored the fullness, roundness, softness of a heavier woman's body. The feel of Paris's thick thighs wrapped around his waist last night had been intoxicating. His cock hardened further, pushing into her back. He stilled as she pushed her hips back into him. Was she awake or reacting in her sleep? Xavier waited for any further indication, but she didn't move again. Sighing with relief that he hadn't woken her, yet mildly disappointed that it hadn't been an invitation for something more, Xavier decided that he wasn't going to get back to sleep and turned over to check the time. It was just before six. Coffee was needed.

Slowly he rolled away from the inviting body of Paris and slid out of bed. Quietly as he could he drew the curtains closed and opened his closet door to find a t-shirt for Paris to wear when she got up. He draped it on the end of the bed and scooped up the two towels they had used last night, dumping them in the laundry basket on his way out to the kitchen. He pulled on the pajama pants he had brought out with him and turned on the coffee pod machine. As he didn't want to wake Paris, he used the main bathroom rather than the ensuite. He had a quick shower and brushed his teeth. He smiled to himself as he noticed Paris's clothing folded on the edge of the tub. Her bathers hanging over the side to dry. For some unknown reason, the sight brought him happiness. After only two weeks he was smitten with more intense emotions than he had for any other woman he had dated. Maybe his parents had been telling the truth that when you know, you know.

He made his coffee, hoping that the pod machine didn't wake Paris, before taking the blanket he kept on the side of his couch and wrapping it around his shoulders, and slowly opening the balcony door so he could watch the sky lighten as twilight faded and the sun rose. The air outside still held its heat from the day before and Xavier put the blanket aside as he sat at the small table. He sipped his coffee and allowed his mind to relax, not focusing on anything in particular. His life was good.

The sun made its way above the horizon and the sounds of people moving around filled the air, as the restaurant owners in the strip below began to arrive to start their day.

Sundays were always busy, but on this perfect summer morning, they would be more so.

A small cough behind Xavier announced that Paris was up. "Good morning," she said brightly.

Xavier unfolded himself from the chair and turned to find her standing there, her hair still messy and wearing only his t-shirt. Thoughts of inviting her back to his bed crossed his mind.

"Good morning. Would you like a tea or coffee? I was just about to make another cup."

"Coffee would be great."

As he walked by her he spontaneously swept her up and planted a hard kiss on her mouth. It appeared she was irresistible to him. Paris laughed with delight until his mouth closed on hers and she wound her arms around his neck moving to stand on her toes to reach him better. With effort, he broke the kiss and placed a quick peck on her fore-head before continuing into the kitchen to make her coffee.

Paris pulled her top down and it was only then did Xavier belatedly realize that she wore nothing underneath. It took all his effort not to abandon the making of her coffee to ravish her here, up against the kitchen bench. *She needs to shower and brush her teeth,* he told himself, *you don't need to overwhelm her.*

"Can I ask you a question?" She broke into his thoughts.

"Always."

"It's probably not politically correct," she warned, her voice the most uncertain he had heard.

Xavier stopped and looked at her seriously. "As far as I am concerned, it is only politically incorrect when there is evil intent behind it and you have absolutely none of that."

He smiled at her for reassurance. "Though, I have a fair idea it will only be about one of two things."

"Really?" Paris raised her eyebrows in surprise. "What do you think I am going to ask about?"

"You are either going to ask me about my birthmark or you are going to ask me why I am so tall." Xavier knew that he was right by the look on her face.

Paris started to laugh. "I am curious about your birthmark and probably would have asked about it at some point, but yes I wanted to know why you are so tall."

"Let me make you a coffee first and then I will tell you the tale."

"Oooh, a tale." Paris laughed.

Efficiently, Xavier made them both a pod coffee and led her back out to the balcony. He found Paris staring at him as he got comfortable in his seat, turning to face her a little more. "What?" he asked.

Her grin was wicked, which made his groin tighten. "You are very distracting without your shirt on."

"I am assuming that is a good thing?"

"Oh, yes, a very good thing unless you need me to focus properly." Paris winked, making him laugh.

"Should I put a top on?"

"Fuck no."

He laughed harder.

"Your tale, please. I promise to stop ogling and try to listen."

"When you asked why am I so tall, I am guessing you meant to put on the end, 'for an Asian man'?"

Paris flushed prettily and Xavier took it as a yes.

"Did you not wonder why I also had a very non-Asian name?"

"I hadn't thought about it. But now you bring it up, Xavier Worthington is about as non-Asian as it comes."

"My middle name is Aki, also odd, because Chinese people don't typically have middle names."

"I like it."

"Thank you. Anyway, while most Asian races are shorter, Koreans are quite tall." He took a sip of his coffee, sighing at the wonderful aroma and flavor.

"I didn't know that."

"A lot of people don't. We sort of all get lumped together. Anyway, that has nothing to do with my story."

"You aren't Korean?"

"Nope, one of my ancestors was Australian. A very tall young man, who fought in World War II in Singapore and became a Prisoner of War where he was starved and ill-treated by the Japanese for over a year. At the end of the war, he was too sick to travel home immediately and was cared for and nursed back to health by the local doctor and his daughter. By the time he had healed enough to travel, he had fallen in love with the doctor's daughter and chose to stay in Singapore and help rebuild the nation as he had been a carpenter before he joined the war. The soldier and daughter were married three months after meeting."

"Three months?" Paris spluttered as she put down her coffee. "That seems awfully quick."

"It has become a bit of a family tradition."

"So, they were your?"

"My great grandparents."

"It is a wonderful story."

"Thank you."

"And you said it is a family tradition. What does that mean?"

"My family tends to find their soulmate and fall in love when they are quite young and are usually married within six months."

He watched Paris swallow hard and wondered whether it had been wise to share the story after all. Most people he told it to found it romantic. She did not appear to think it was. Then again, this was the first woman he had told it to that he was seriously infatuated with. He had to admit he was hoping for a more positive response.

"Your whole family?"

"Yes, even my sister found love at twenty and was married only a few months later."

"Is there much expectation for you to do the same?"

Xavier laughed, attempting to show that this was supposed to be a light-hearted conversation. He was most certainly regretting starting it now. "Well, obviously, I am far older than my family members, but I do believe that there is no need for conventional waiting times if you are certain"

He decided against telling her that his mother had spent the past ten years attempting to set him up with who she thought would be suitable for her son. As soon as he had completed high school and had turned eighteen the subtle set-ups had begun. Now they weren't subtle, as her desperation increased.

Paris was quiet as she drank her coffee and watched the seagulls fight for scraps of food. He wondered what she was thinking, but was too afraid to ask.

The moment was interrupted by his doorbell. Xavier checked his watch; it was just after nine. Who could be turning up this early on a Sunday morning?

"You expecting someone?" Paris asked.

"No, and not this early on a Sunday."

As he made his way back into the lounge area, the doorbell buzzed again. "Just a minute," he called out and headed to his room. He needed to get a top on. He wasn't comfortable answering the door with a bare chest. Paris followed him into his room and took her straw bag from the corner. "I better put some pants on. Can I use the bathroom again, please?"

"Of course you can, you don't need to ask." Xavier gave her a quick peck on the forehead as he went by.

Xavier looked through the peephole to discover a woman standing on the other side. He had no idea who she was. Xavier opened the door and smiled politely. "Hello?"

She was a smidge taller than Paris and pencil-thin. Her smart-looking outfit looked more like she was heading to the office rather than spending a Sunday relaxing in the hot summer of Melbourne. A white chiffon sleeveless shirt, paired with a black flared mid-length skirt, and patent leather black flats completed her look. She wore her long, straight black hair out, but the front was held back by a wide white headband. The look was conservative and Xavier started to feel ill as he realized why the young woman was standing at his door. On schedule, his phone beeped and he knew who it was sending him a text.

The young woman held out her hand and Xavier took it. She gave it a weak shake. "Good morning, I hope I haven't disturbed you, but your mother wanted me to introduce myself as I have just moved to Melbourne. She thought we could have breakfast seeing as it is just below your building." She spoke quietly, her English perfect and only held a vague accent. Like him, she was clearly educated from an early age in an English-speaking environment.

"Nice to meet you..." He left it there, hoping she would realize that she had not given him her name.

"Oh, how silly of me. I am Jin." She looked up at him and he could see her interest in her brown eyes. What had his mother said that would make this young woman turn up at a stranger's door and announce they should go out for breakfast?

Xavier's phone beeped again. His mother being impatient and wanting to know what was occurring was his guess.

"It is lovely to meet you, Jin, but there has been a misunderstanding," Xavier said it softly, hoping that a quieter voice would let her down gently. "I can't have breakfast with you."

"Yes, he can," Paris announced behind him.

He turned to find her fully dressed in a blue high waisted sundress, with a v-neckline that exposed enough of her breasts to make him struggle to keep his eyes where they were supposed to be. "But we have plans," he announced to both of them. Xavier felt confused. Why was Paris doing this?

"I have a lot of work and we can catch up another time. You and Jin go have breakfast like your mother wishes." Paris gave him a quick kiss on the cheek before stepping through the open door. "Thanks for letting me crash here," she announced. "Have a great breakfast you two." And with that she was off down the hall, heading toward the elevator.

"Well, isn't she sweet," Jin stepped into the apartment without being invited and alarm bells went off. "I'll wait while you get dressed."

Xavier closed the door as his phone began to ring. He felt sick. What he wanted to do was chase Paris down the hallway, but his good manners kept him dealing with Jin.

"You should probably answer that. I don't think your mother is going away until you tell her I am here and you are taking me out." Jin spoke with a confidence he wasn't expecting as most of the women his mother picked were far less forward—his mother had upped her game. Suddenly he felt as if the walls were closing in and he was trapped.

CHAPTER EIGHT
PARIS

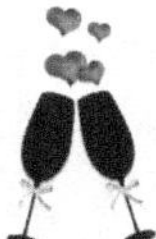

Please answer your phone.

The text came through after she had declined his call twice. Paris pursed her lips as she considered her choices. She longed to pick up the phone and hear his voice but she fought against the want. She could still hear Jin's voice announcing who she was and that his mother had sent her. Regardless of what she had said, the intention for her arriving so early on a Sunday morning was clear. Paris had felt crushed when she had seen the girl; tiny, thin, and perfectly presented. She had just reacted without truly thinking about the situation and had got dressed and fled rather than take the chance that Xavier would ask her to leave.

Abruptly it made sense as to why she had run rather than wait to see how it unfolded. *You were scared that he was going to ask you to leave and choose Jin,* she thought to herself. *And really, why would he ask you to stay when he already got what he wanted from you and he had a willing date with his mother's approval?* It was a sickening thought.

And she wouldn't answer his calls because she didn't want to know who he had chosen.

"You do know you are being ridiculous, right?" she said to the quiet of her unit. "He has been very clear that he likes you." *And you like him,* she admitted to herself. Paris also acknowledged deep down that if pushed she would have to admit that it was more than just like—she was smitten. After only a few weeks it was a lot to experience so quickly, especially for one not used to any relationship. She had been hoping he would bring up the conversation to define their relationship, but that had not happened and Paris was too inexperienced and nervous to do it herself.

Her phone began to ring again and her stomach lurched with a mixture of longing and fear. *For fuck's sake, just answer it,* her brain yelled at her. *You won't know anything until you talk to him.*

With a lot of misgivings, Paris hit the answer button. "Hello."

"Hey." His voice was soft and her heart melted. "Are you okay? You left so quickly."

Shit, she hadn't thought about what she would say was her reason for running out. "I had a few things to do and I thought I would give you the chance to have breakfast with your mother's gift." It came out before she had a chance to sensor it. Paris cringed at her neediness.

Xavier was silent for a moment and Paris wondered if he was deciding to hang up rather than deal with her insecurities. "That is an interesting way to put it." His voice remained calm and soft.

"Does it happen often?" *Shut up,* her mental voice screeched at her.

"Yes and no." Xavier paused and Paris wondered what he was about to say. "It's not a conversation I want to have over the phone."

"Oh." Paris was lost for words. That was not the answer she was expecting. He was so freakin calm and she was a bundle of insecure nerves. "Did you have breakfast with her?" *What the actual fuck is wrong with you?* If her inner voice had eyes she would be receiving a death stare, she was sure of it.

"No. I was hoping to spend the day with you after such a wonderful day yesterday, but you left before I could ask you or explain that to Jin." Paris irrationally hated the way his voice caressed Jin's name. *You need to get a grip, you are acting like a love-sick idiot.* Xavier went on, oblivious to her turmoil. "I was going to ask you to come to dinner to meet my best friend, her wife, and their baby tonight."

Paris felt foolish. "Oh. That sounds fun." She was grateful that he could not see her blush as she realized how worked up she had become over the situation.

"I just have a favor to ask." His voice sounded hesitant.

Her mind jumped to several scenarios, each one worse than the other. He wanted them to pretend to be friends. He wanted her to not mention that his mother was setting him up on dates. He wanted her to forget last night and really just be friends. That one made her feel ill.

"Would it be possible for you to tone down the language tonight?"

"Sorry?"

"And the innuendo?"

Her temper was quick to flare. "Would you like to

repeat that? I think I misunderstood what you said." Her voice was cold and flat.

Xavier coughed slightly. "It's not a big thing. My friends are fairly straight-laced in that they don't swear."

"I can't believe you just asked me to change who I am to fit in with your friends. Should they not accept me for who I am?"

"You just tend to swear a lot." His voice had taken on a slightly desperate tone as he tried to explain.

"So, is it really that you don't like it and want me to not swear so much? And you are using your friends as an excuse to tell me?"

"No, maybe. I am not sure." He stopped.

She waited.

"I am not used to a woman swearing so much and I know my friends aren't. I just wanted to stop any embarrassment."

Paris exploded. "Embarrassment? Who the hell do you think you are? Are your friends so precious that they have never heard bad language before or make judgments when they hear curse words spoken? I thought you liked me just the way I was, but no, it turns out you want to change me too. Am I not good enough?" It stung her to say it.

"Paris, I didn't mean to upset you, it's the last thing I want to do. I never said I wanted you to change."

"Maybe you should have thought about that before you asked me to." Paris took in a deep breath and with effort, reigned in her temper. "You know what the worst thing is?" Her voice caught and she willed herself not to cry. "I would never swear around a child. I was raised better than that."

"I am sorry, I am an idiot. Of course, you have." Xavier

sounded upset, but she didn't care; he was not who she thought he was.

"Thank you for the invitation but I won't be joining you and your friends for dinner tonight. Goodbye, Xavier."

She hung up before he could say anything that would hurt her further. Tears began to fall as she tried to fathom how the conversation had become so messy. He had hurt her feelings and she had retaliated without pausing to consider anything. She had truly never been so irrational.

Xavier

"Where is Paris?" May demanded as soon as she was able to quiet the barking Angus and open the front door.

"She couldn't make it," Xavier said as he kissed his friend's cheek and handed over a bottle of wine.

"I hope everything is okay?"

"Yes, yes, all fine. She just had something else going on."

"And I was looking forward to meeting her." May led him down to the kitchen area. The house smelt wonderful.

"What's for dinner? It smells great." Xavier hoped to change subjects; he didn't want to talk about Paris. He was upset with how their conversation had turned out and he was confused by how she had ended the phone call. Her goodbye had sounded too final.

"Bruchetta for an entree with Chicken Alfredo for main and a chocolate flan for dessert."

"You went fancy."

"It was no trouble, you know I love to cook for friends."

"I told you not to go to any trouble."

May laughed. "I didn't."

"Mmmm... did you make the pasta and bread from scratch?"

"Well, yes."

"And the pastry for the flan?" Xavier watched her shrug and knew that to be a yes.

"I was hoping to impress your friend. You have never brought anyone here for me to meet before, so I figured it must be serious."

It was his turn to shrug. Xavier was uncomfortable with the way the conversation was going.

"Xavier..." May began, but he was saved by Taree carrying out his Godson, Seb.

"And here is Uncle Xavier," Taree announced as she handed Seb over to Xavier without anyone asking. She kissed him on the cheek. "But where is his special friend?"

Xavier looked down at the gorgeous baby boy and was shocked to find that the first thing he thought about was what his and Paris's children would look like. "Hey there, handsome." He smiled down at the sleeping child and resisted the urge to squeeze him. "Have you been good for your Mums?"

He looked up to find both women smiling fondly at him. "What?" he asked suspiciously.

"You are a natural," Taree announced.

"I only like him because he is yours," he defended himself half-heartedly. "Why don't you pour me a wine while I take care of your progeny?" Xavier was doing well with the deflection.

"Sure," Taree said brightly. "But that won't stop me from asking about the absence of your special friend."

May laughed but didn't stop her wife from continuing.

Taree got out the bottle opener while May took several glasses out of the cupboard. "Well?" Taree prompted. "Where is Paris?"

"She couldn't make it. I left it too late to ask and she had something else planned," he lied.

"Xavier, do you expect me to believe that?"

"Yes." He straightened indignantly. "Why would I lie?"

"I am not sure, but you have never been very good at it. You try to avoid rather than an outright lie."

Xavier ran his hand gently across Seb's perfect scalp. He bent to smell him. How did babies always smell so good when all they did was puke and poop? "My day started perfectly and has gradually gotten worse because I handled everything poorly. And now I am unsure if Paris said goodbye for now or goodbye forever and the forever is scaring me. This is all new." He wanted to flop down in the chair but sat carefully as to not wake the sleeping baby.

May handed him a glass of wine and clinked her glass to his. "To the mistakes we make, and owning and fixing them."

Xavier took a sip before groaning. "That sounds difficult."

Taree came and clinked her glass to his and her wife's. "Difficult, absolutely, but for the right person so worth it."

"The question is, is she the right person?"

There it was out in the open, the question he had been avoiding. Was Paris the one? Or was that added pressure to make her the one because of his family? Was he trying to avoid his feeling because he was scared or was he trying to feel more than he did?

"I think she is, but that terrifies me because that means I could lose her which means I think I am trying too hard and have now made everything worse because I want it to be perfect." He took a gulp and sighed with frustration.

May sat down opposite him and smiled kindly. "I am happy for you, but it will only work if you are open with her."

"I may have been too open with her."

Taree sat next to her wife and groaned. "What did you do?"

"Well, the morning started well. She stayed over and we were enjoying a coffee on the balcony when we were interrupted by the doorbell. It seems my mother has grown desperate and is no longer waiting for me to go home to set up dates, she is now sending them to my door on any pretense they can come up with."

Both women gasped. "She did not!" Taree yelped loudly enough that Seb became restless with the noise.

Xavier rocked and cooed at him for a moment until he settled. He looked up to find May scowling at him. "He doesn't calm that quickly for me."

For the first time since Paris had left his apartment that morning he laughed. "It would appear I can't make any women happy in my life."

"Both of you stop feeling so sorry for yourself," admonished Taree. "You make my head hurt. Now, get back to your story."

May stood and moved around the kitchen bench. "Keep

talking, I just have to turn the oven on and put the water on to boil."

"Jin was a perfectly acceptable candidate who I was expected to take to breakfast, and she was far more forward than the usual girls. Paris must have heard enough, and before I could explain she left on the pretense that she had things to do."

"And you let her go?"

"Well, yes, Jin was standing at my door." Realization dawned on Xavier. "Bugger. I should have chased her."

"Of course you should have. Who was the more important person in that situation?"

"Paris."

"She probably thinks you chose Jin." Taree pointed out unhelpfully as he could see that now.

"So, you rang and apologized?"

"Well, yes, but now I am thinking not for the right thing. She was quick to ask if I had gone out with her and she said a few odd things."

"Xavier, seriously. Have I not taught you anything about women?" May asked as she returned to the table. "She was trying to figure out where she stands with you, as I am assuming you have not had any serious discussion about your feelings?"

The phone call was all falling into place now. He had handled everything wrong, what she needed was reassurance and he had asked her to change.

"She swears a lot. Drops the F-word frequently and sprinkles other words throughout." He looked down at Seb rather than face the wrath he knew was about to unfold. "She agreed to come to dinner tonight and then I asked her to not curse while here." He winced and waited for the outburst.

"Why on earth would you do that?" May asked.

Taree laughed, which was not the response he was expecting. "You truly do some stupid things. Finally, you find a woman who makes you happy and you go and sabotage it."

"Why would you think we would care about that?" May asked.

All the questions were making him feel a little under siege. "I don't know now. The swearing does bother me a little, but I just thought with Seb and all."

"Seb is a baby, we don't need to worry about swearing for quite some time. And I am certain she would tone it down around children. She sounds like a wonderful person," May said.

"That's what she pointed out before telling me she thought it best she didn't come to dinner and then she said goodbye. It felt so final." He didn't like admitting that, but it was true.

"What do you want, Xavier? A Paris that swears a bit too much occasionally or no Paris?" Taree asked the direct question, she was always good with those.

"I want Paris."

"Then man up and fix it."

CHAPTER NINE
PARIS

The early evening sun felt delightful on her skin as she pulled the hair from her eyes, as it had been whipping around as they drove in Xavier's convertible. He laughed and squeezed her hand as they sat at the traffic lights and she whooped like a child with the carefree feeling she felt. It had been a miserable few days after their argument on Sunday. Paris had fretted that she had pushed him away and that he wouldn't want to see her anymore. She struggled to find her feet with him, he sent her spinning in a way no one had before. She longed for him, thought about him touching her, obsessed about him being with her, and she fought the urge to see him every second she could. Then they had argued and Paris had become a barely functioning human. Work had been her saving grace, as her workload picked up as she finalized so many tiny details before the overseas students began to arrive after the Australia Day weekend, in two days. It was her favorite time at work, as it could be so satisfying, but it was also the most chaotic. It had kept her mind occupied most of the days, but at night, when she was alone, nothing could stop her from thinking about Xavier and what he was doing. She knew he had several flights earlier in the week, but all she could focus on was if his mother set up other women for him when he stayed in Singapore... it had made her insides ache to think about it. Mandi had urged her to contact him, but Paris felt that it was up to him as he had caused the argument.

Thankfully, that morning he had rung and explained that he was about to fly back to Melbourne and if she was willing, he would like to make it up to her and try again, by taking her to his friend's place for dinner. They both wanted to meet her and had told him how much of a fool he had been. He had then apologized. Paris had forgiven him instantly, holding her tongue but knowing that he probably deserved a minor apology for her over-reaction. For some reason, she found it hard to admit she may have been wrong too.

They pulled up to a beautiful house, and Xavier pressed a button so the roof could rise and reattach itself to the car. He got out and came around to her side, he opened the door and held out a hand to help her out of the low-lying car. She tried not to give an unladylike grunt as she climbed out. With a slow grin, he pinned her to the side of the car and kissed her soundly. His tongue finding hers before sliding across her bottom lip. "I missed you," he whispered into her ear and then planted a kiss just under her earlobe. This sent a delightful shiver across her shoulders.

Paris pulled his head down for another kiss. "How about we skip dinner and go do bad things to each other instead?"

He lifted an eyebrow. "I have no idea what you are talking about." He went to kiss her again.

"Are you two just about finished?" a female voice called out.

Paris blushed and laughed when she saw that Xavier's face was as red as she guessed hers was. "That will be Taree. May is a little more reserved."

Xavier took her hand and pulled her toward the house. They were greeted by an average height, slender, Asian woman with short-cropped hair and the most delicately gold-brown hooded eyes. Paris was in awe of her beauty. She had an open smile and was accompanied by a jumping small dog. She gave Xavier a warm hug, and Paris experienced an unreasonable surge of jealousy, before turning to Paris. "I am Taree, welcome to our home." She embraced Paris and as she stepped back gave her an obvious wink. "So, Xavier, Paris can't swear around us, but you can accost her out the front of our house?"

Paris laughed as his face flamed.

Taree was joined at the door by another Asian woman, but she had a fuller figure, broader planes on her face, and a comely appearance. She carried a baby up on her shoulder and gently rubbed its back. "Stop teasing him."

"But you should have seen him, mauling Paris in the middle of the street."

Paris was enjoying the friendly teasing but decided to rescue him. She held out the box of chocolates she had brought to Taree but faced May. "I am Paris, it is nice to finally meet you."

"Welcome, Paris. Come in."

Paris followed May into the gorgeous home. Paris

couldn't help but smile at the beautiful baby as his huge eyes peaked over his mother's shoulder as they walked down the hallway. She longed to ask to hold him but thought it might seem rude as they had just met. They came out into an enormous kitchen, with a rack hanging from the ceiling filled with copper pots and pans. Her mother had always wanted one, but her father had claimed it was a dust collector. But these pans gleamed in the rays of the early evening sun. "I thought with the weather so wonderful today that we could sit outside tonight and have a barbecue," May announced as she moved to the open sliding door and they stepped out into a lush courtyard, filled with green potted ferns and hanging baskets of what Paris guessed to be herbs, which would make sense as May was a chef.

A gleaming silver barbecue sat to one side, while in the center was an eight-seater square table with pretty citronella candles in the middle to help keep the mosquitos away. The table was set with clear, crystal glasses, a white linen table cloth and matching napkins, and fine white china. It was the fanciest barbecue setting Paris had ever experienced.

"A glass of white wine, Paris?" Taree called from the kitchen as everyone began to sit.

"Yes, please, but can I also have a glass of water?" Paris was nervous. She didn't want to drink too much, as when she got tipsy she always swore more and she was very aware of making a good impression tonight, knowing that Xavier had told them why they had fought.

"Xavier?"

"Water and wine are good for me too, thank you," Xavier called out.

Taree came out carrying an ice bucket with a bottle of opened wine in it, plus a glass jug of water with ice cubes. She poured drinks for everyone.

"You going to give Seb over, May?" Xavier asked, his hands reaching out greedily for the baby.

"Once he has burped he is all yours. Unless you want to risk getting thrown up on?"

"No, no, all good here." Xavier quickly turned his reaching hands into palms out, as if that would keep the expected spit-up at bay.

"Xavier tells me that you were the one behind the incredible meals on New Year's Eve," Paris opened the conversation. "And he is trying to convince me that he was helpful in the kitchen that night."

"Yes, and he was doing an amazing job at helping me until he spotted you, then he became useless." May laughed.

"Hey, why are we trying to embarrass Xavier tonight?"

This made everyone laugh. "Because you are such an easy target," answered Taree.

"So, you enjoyed New Year?" Taree asked Paris and it was her turn to blush.

"It got better as the night went on," she answered with a smile at Xavier.

"Did you make any resolutions before our hero here claimed you from the dance floor?" May asked.

"I don't do resolutions. I think it just sets you up for failure. No one ever keeps them and I just can't think of any that I want to stick to to break my own rule," she explained.

Taree grinned at her. "Well, finally a sensible human. I totally agree. I don't have resolutions either, but I do goals."

"I hadn't thought about setting goals, rather than making grand statements."

Taree nodded. "I set two goals for the year. One frivolous and fun, and one serious that I want to achieve."

Paris liked the idea of that. It was something she could get behind. "It's a shame New Year has gone. Goals are definitely more my style."

Seb interrupted the conversation with a loud and satisfying burp, which brought the attention back to the baby.

⚘

"Thank you for having me, I had a wonderful evening." Paris kissed both the women and hugged them. "Seb is adorable."

Xavier followed her in, giving each of his friends a parting kiss and hug, thanking them for the great food, and making fun of him in front of Paris when he was trying to impress her.

"It was our pleasure. We hope to do it again soon." Taree smirked and made a hasty retreat into the house as May closed the door.

Paris took Xavier's hand as they walked down the gravel driveway listening to May pretend to threaten to return the dog to the pound as Angus barked at the front window. As they reached the car and Xavier opened her door, Paris hoped for a repeat performance of when they had arrived, but he was a perfect gentleman and escorted her into the car and closed the door behind her.

As Paris settled into the plush leather seat and the car pulled away from the curb, she thought about the wonderful evening and how welcoming his friends had been. "Your friends are lovely."

"They think you are great."

"I can't believe that Taree had a baby like six weeks ago. She looks incredible."

"Motherhood suits her. May is having a harder time adjusting."

"To be so thin after giving birth, she is so lucky." Paris was envious. "Both of them are beautiful, but I felt like a huge heifer standing next to the petite Taree. What is her heritage?"

"Taree is half Thai, half Australian. May is Malaysian," explained Xavier as he pulled up to a set of lights. "Did you enjoy the food?"

"Fuck, yes. I've never had salmon on the barbie before." It was good to get that *fuck* out. She had not sworn all night. It had been tiring to watch every word, but she had wanted to show Xavier that she was capable of being a little less Aussie country girl.

"You didn't eat much."

Paris had hoped he wouldn't notice. How was she going to answer that without looking silly? "I didn't want them to think I was being a pig."

"No one would have thought you were being a pig. May loves it when people eat her food. Why would they think that?"

Paris looked out the window, watching the trees go by as they neared her flat. "I am fairly sure you know why."

Xavier sighed and they drove along in silence for several minutes. "Can you just eat the amount you want and be satisfied with the way you look?" he asked softly as they drove along the quiet streets.

Rather than answer, Paris attempted to change the subject. "What are you doing this weekend? Are you working?"

"I am flying out tomorrow and back Saturday, both early flights. I am not sure about the rest of the weekend. Did you have plans?"

"Well, it is Australia Day holiday on Monday so was thinking I might go and visit my parents if you weren't around." What Paris wanted to do was ask him to come with her, but she felt like that would be too early and give him the wrong message.

They pulled up at her house, and she sat and waited for him to come around and help her out of the low car. This time she didn't wait to see what he would do, she took the initiative and pulled him to her by the front of his shirt. She kissed him with the need she had felt growing since that initial kiss when they had arrived at May's house. Paris thought about wrapping her leg around his hips right there and freeing him from his pants so he could take her immediately. Her core burned and her clit throbbed with the idea. Instead, she took his perfect arse in her hands and ground her groin against his, making her want clear.

He broke the kiss but continued to hold her close. He gently kissed a trail of tiny pecks up her nose and across her forehead, before he leaned his forehead against hers. "I can't come in. I have an early flight tomorrow, as it is I am only going to get about six hours sleep." He trailed kisses back down her nose. "Most people want their pilots to be well-rested." His hand moved up her curvy waist and his thumb brushed the side of her breast as he deepened his kiss. She squeezed his arse and circled her hips into his, eliciting a satisfying groan from him.

"Can't you just use autopilot?" she asked as they again paused to catch their breath. She figured this was what frustrated teens felt when they first started making out. It was something she had never experienced before and she had to admit the slow torture of passionate kissing with knowing your wants were not going to be met were tantalizingly fun.

"It doesn't work like that," he responded. "I have to go." He kissed her cheek. "I had a great night." He kissed her other cheek. "Thank you for coming with me." He kissed the tip of her nose. "Next time I want you to be you and eat and swear, just a little." He kissed her forehead.

Paris laughed. "You are being a little bossy." She pulled him to her and placed her head against his hard, perfect chest. He smelled amazing.

"If I had enough time, I would come in and show you just how bossy I can be." He ran his hand over her hair.

His words gave her a thrill. How could someone sound so naughty and yet use no bad language? "Promises, promises," she murmured as she kissed his chest.

Xavier stepped away from her and held out his hand. "I will walk you to your door as long as you don't try to lure me inside."

Paris laughed as she took his hand. "Well, that takes all the fun out of it."

CHAPTER TEN
XAVIER

Not for the first time that day did Xavier wonder why Paris had not invited him to meet her parents. "You seem distracted," his mother commented as the two of them sat down to dinner. "Is it that girl?"

It was only the two of them at the table. His sister and her family were having dinner at her in-laws, his father was at a monthly "business meeting," well that's what he told the family, they all knew he was playing poker at a friend's house, and his grandparents had chosen to eat in their rooms as they were feeling a little under the weather. Xavier didn't blame them, summer in Singapore was humid and exhausting at times, even though they lived in air conditioning throughout the grand house.

It felt odd to sit at the overly large ornate table with only the two of them and a servant hovering nearby. His family was rich, not Crazy Rich Asian rich, but well off. It was something he had kept from Paris, though she must have figured they had some money to be able to send their son to boarding school in another country.

"Xavier?"

"Yes?" He took several scallops from the serving platter the servant offered him.

"The girl?"

"Her name is Paris." He looked meaningfully toward the servant then back at Andrea.

They ate in silence for several minutes. His mother never had an issue discussing things in front of the staff, Xavier did not feel the same way. It would be a stand-off to see if she respected him enough to wait until the servant had left. Another servant carried out a silver tray that held several dishes. They placed fried rice, a pork hot pot, and a seafood birds nest in the center of the two of them. At this point, his mother announced that they would serve themselves and that the staff could eat.

She turned to Xavier. "Tell me about Paris."

"I am sure Jin told you enough." He broke off a piece of the crispy birds nest—it had been his favorite dish since he was a child.

"Jin was upset that you turned down her offer of breakfast," his mother chided.

"I was upset that she turned up without invitation in the first place," Xavier said quietly. "Please don't do that again."

"I just want you to be happy." Andrea flicked her long, straight black hair over a shoulder. She gave him a penetrating look, her brown eyes so much like his own. His mother wore her customary black pants and silk shirt, today it was a deep red and matched her painted lips. She was the picture of understated cool elegance.

"I am happy with my life. What I am not happy with is

your never-ending interference with finding me a wife." He tried to remember that he was a twenty-eight-year-old man, not a small child because that is the way she made him feel. "I like Paris, and Jin turning up almost ruined a perfect weekend."

"The last Caucasian girl you went out with broke your heart," she reminded him.

"I don't think her race had anything to do with it, and no, she didn't. We were friends and we grew to something more, but then it fizzled." He decided that the blunt truth was the only way to get his mother to understand it was time to back off. "I thought I loved her, but now I know different."

"Why don't you like any of the dates I have found for you? They are all lovely, young women." she pushed.

Well, this is about to get awkward, but she is my mother and maybe the truth will help her understand, Xavier tried to cajole himself into revealing the truth. He needed her to stop, he didn't want to lose Paris because of his mother. "The women you choose are all beautiful and kind and honorable." He bit his lip before he went on, he could feel the color rise in his face. "But I like sassy, funny, curvy women. The women you pick never show me anything other than what I am supposed to see. Though Jin had a little more spark than normal. Paris is real, swear words, body anxiety, and all." And with those words spoken it hit him. He had been trying to fix her into the mold his mother had been presenting him.

His job meant he had to be clinical and a clear thinker when it came to problem-solving. He was used to applying that to all aspects of his life. It turned out that you couldn't apply that to a complicated, messy human who had their own emotions and fears. He felt a surge of panic as he realized that unless he started telling her how he felt instead of trying to fix her, he would lose her. Maybe that was why he hadn't got an invite, maybe she needed time to think about how she felt? This made him more distressed. He needed to see her to clear up any confusion, and to ask for forgiveness for not being there and instead trying to change her by dismissing her valid feelings.

"Xavier?" By the tone of his mother's voice, she had been waiting for an answer to a question for some time.

"I apologize. I just had an unsettling realization and I didn't hear you." He continued with *honesty is the best policy* with his mother, surprised she had not rebuffed his words. "What did you say?"

"It sounds to me like you care for this Paris greatly, but does she care for you as much?"

"I thought she did, but I have made a few silly choices and have not supported her as much as I should and now I am not so sure."

His mother stopped eating and brought her hands up to her head and cradled her head, shaking it slowly. "Men," she stated simply.

"Mum." Xavier was shocked by her response, it was unexpected.

"Two things, my beautiful son. One, be honest. If you were honest with me from the beginning, I would never have foisted all those slim, quiet girls on you. You are quiet and gentle and I thought that is what appealed to you."

"You would have just foisted a different type of woman on me," he pointed out.

Surprisingly, she laughed. "Well, yes, probably, but we are not talking about me." She took a sip of her water before going on. "You need to be honest with Paris. She can't guess how you are feeling with stupid men clues. Speak up."

Xavier couldn't hide his shock. His mother had never spoken to him with such clarity before. Their relationship had always been more superficial than his other family members, though he rarely spoke about his feelings with anyone but May and Taree. He was almost afraid to ask what her second thing was.

"When did you meet?" she asked.

"At a New Year's Eve party that May was catering."

His mother's perfect eyebrows raised in unison and a smile spread across her broad features. "Twenty-six days then?"

Xavier was confused for a moment. "Pardon?"

"So the family tradition holds."

Xavier's brown eyes widened as he understood what she was implying. "I am older than everyone else was," he pointed out, trying to divert the line of thought he knew his mother was heading to.

She reached out and took his hand. "It is good to see that you don't deny you love her, now you need to go and tell her."

His face fell as he registered the words his mother had spoken, they were not what he had expected. Xavier had expected resistance from Andrea, but obviously, she had truly only wanted him to find love, and now she felt he had, she would encourage him to follow it. He did love Paris, she was right for him in every way, but he had not spoken the truth. And to make matters worse he had asked her to change or then dismissed her fears and she had not asked him to go with her to meet her parents, which had made him worry, but he had not voiced it. "I can't go tell her, she is visiting her parents this weekend," he explained.

"It is only Friday night, you will be home tomorrow at lunchtime," his mother pointed out. "I am sure you can figure it out if she is as important as you claim."

"Maybe..."

"Is there something wrong with your eggs, Honey?"

"No, they are great, why?"

"Because your fork has been chasing them around the plate for the last five minutes while you stare off into space."

Paris sighed heavily and put a forkful of scrambled eggs in her mouth. She had slept late in the hope that she could hide from her emotions but it hadn't worked. The first thing she thought of when she had woken was Xavier and why he hadn't made any contact with her since Thursday night. Her mother had suggested they go into town and have lunch at the newest trendy cafe that her mother had declared was fancy because they served all-day breakfast. It had been a pleasant way to spend an hour, catching her mother up on all the office gossip and Mandi's love life, until her mother had received a text and apologized, explaining that she had just become the president of the local art society and they were in the middle of organizing their first exhibition and she couldn't not answer her messages. This had given Paris too much time to think and what she discovered hadn't made her happy. Why was she waiting for him to phone her? He was working, she wasn't. If she wanted to be in the relationship and show him that she was interested, maybe she should be a bit more proactive. *I hope I am not too late*, she was thinking when her mother stopped texting and asked her about her meal.

Paris caught sight of a young couple walking down the street, arm in arm, chatting. She quickly looked away, hoping they wouldn't see her. The young woman was gorgeous in every way and the man was the quintessential perfect-looking country boy, but both were cruel and had made her late high school years a living hell. She picked up her tea cup and concentrated on sipping the tangy liquid and deliberately not looking out the window.

Kathleen put her phone down and picked up her coffee mug. "Would you like to tell me about him?" Her mother smiled knowingly at her.

"Him?" Paris was all innocence.

"Oh, Honey, no one acts this way without there being a guy involved."

Paris dropped the innocent eyes and frowned. "I didn't know I was being obvious."

"Your brothers and father don't have a clue, but I know what I am looking for."

Paris pushed her half-eaten meal to the side, there was no point in just playing with it. "His name is Xavier and I met him on New Year's Eve at the work party."

"He works with you?"

"No, his friend was catering and he went along to give her a hand and to keep her company." She thought back to the night and her body grew warm and her stomach developed butterflies. "I was trying to sneak off to the bathroom when midnight hit, as everyone was slow dancing or making out and I didn't want to stand out. I thought he was just being nice when he asked me to dance. But then we talked for hours and he asked me out for lunch the next day before explaining that he was a pilot who had just returned to Melbourne." Paris took a sip of her lemon tea and waited for her mother to say something.

"That sounds romantic. Tell me more about him."

"He is kind, intelligent, generous, and fucking hot. Like to die for handsome."

Kathleen frowned at the swearing but refrained from chastising her. "That handsome, huh?"

"You know the guy out of Last Christmas?"

Paris's mother was a big movie buff, she loved all the arts. "Yes, Henry something. Just been cast in the new Jane Austen adaption"

"Yeah, him hot. Tall, built, and beautiful."

"So what is the problem?"

Paris let out a pent-up breath with a hiss. "He makes me completely irrational. I can't think straight, I leap to conclusions." She fiddled with her teaspoon. "He brings up all my insecurities and yet he accepts me for me... though he would like me to tone the cursing down a tad."

"Still waiting to hear what the issue is."

"I just told you." Paris tried to keep the exasperation out of her voice.

"Sounds to me like you are in love with him."

"Don't talk crazy. Why would he love me?"

"I didn't say he loved you, I said you loved him," her

mother pointed out. "And I like anyone that is going to help you stop swearing so much."

"Yes, I thought you might say that."

"Have you told him how you feel?"

"No, it hasn't come up."

Kathleen rolled her eyes to the ceiling. "Hard conversations don't just come up, one of you has to be brave enough to put yourself out there. Be vulnerable." Her mother's laser blue eyes looked at her. "I know you have been deeply hurt in the past but you have to let him in, show him how you feel, and tell him."

Paris nodded. "Don't you think it is all a bit quick? What happens if I have fallen for him because he is the first guy that has truly thought I was attractive?"

"You are looking for faults that aren't there because you are scared. I get that, but don't ruin something that sounds incredible by second-guessing his or your motives." Her mother reached across the small table and cupped Paris's cheek. "Honey, you are a beautiful woman inside and out and it sounds like you have met someone who thinks the same. Sometimes falling in love takes time and sometimes it just takes an instant. Either way, it is a magnificent thing and should be cherished."

Her mother's phone interrupted any further conversation as she leaped on it. Paris almost laughed at how eager her mother was to answer the message when usually Kathleen was the first to tell any family member off for looking at their phone while sitting at the table. Paris thought about pulling her phone out and messaging Xavier as she checked the time on the pretty pink duck clock on the wall. It was almost half-past two, he would have flown in a few hours ago. She wondered what he was doing and for some reason, a picture of Jin popped into her head. *I do need to tell him how I feel or I am going to drive myself crazy not knowing what is happening between the two of us. But not now, do it when no one is around because if I am wrong and he laughs at me, I don't need witnesses to my misery.*

Kathleen put her phone down and grinned weirdly. "Turns out your prince can't live without you and has contacted one of your brother's via messenger to get an address and ask you if it is okay to visit as he couldn't get hold of you for the last few hours."

Paris frowned and picked up her bag, and after a thorough search, she discovered that her phone was not there. "Shit."

"I suggest you stop swearing and we get your bum back to the house to tidy up." Kathleen wrinkled her nose. "Have you even had a shower today?"

Paris stood quickly—she was flustered and thrilled.

"He will be here in an hour unless you ring to tell him not to come. I suggest you make up your mind to shower or call."

The afternoon heat was oppressive as Paris sat on the porch that surrounded the family's farmhouse, waiting for Xavier to arrive. The ice cubes in her iced tea had long melted, and condensation pooled on the rooster coaster it rested on. She was attempting to look relaxed and nonchalant when underneath, her heart lurched as she kept imagining every sound she heard to be his car coming up the tree-lined driveway. Paris checked her phone again to make certain he hadn't tried to call or message. She hoped he hadn't got lost.

Paris was still astounded at the text she had read when they had returned from all-day breakfast at the fancy cafe. It had been far more direct than she was used to from Xavier.

Hi Paris,

I have just walked in the door (to another smelly bin—when will I learn?) and everything is quiet and lonely. I would like to see you—no, I need to see you. I have never wanted anything more than to kiss you right now. I know you are with your family, and I am not sure why I didn't get an invitation to come with you—I am trying not to overthink it. Please call or message me back to say if it is okay for me to come to visit today. I have the next few days off, so you can spend the rest of the weekend showing me where you grew up—I would love to see that part of you.

Waiting to hear from you,

Your Xavier xox

Hi again,

You haven't answered and I am assuming it is because you haven't read the text yet. I don't know why, but I need to see you. I am going to throw caution to the wind and do something I never thought I was capable of. I am going to message a stranger (your brother, Kent) on

Facebook and ask for your address. If you don't want me to come then please let me know, I will turn around and come home if necessary.

Your Xavier xox

On my way,

Your Xavier xox

Paris jumped and gave a squeak of fright as her phone pinged as she was holding it while reading his texts for the umpteenth time. A picture slowly loaded of the family's rooster-shaped letter box—her mother had a thing for roosters—and Paris felt her stomach flip flop.

Here,

Your Xavier xox

His car could now be heard over the typical farm noises and Paris stood and straightened her white sun dress, pulling the ponytail that held her thick auburn hair a little tighter. Her parents joined her on the porch to greet their unexpected but welcome guest. As Xavier's car pulled up, she noted that he had the top-up. Today was too hot to drive exposed to the Australian sun.

Paris led her parents down the three steps as Xavier got out of his car. It took all her strength not to throw herself into his arms and declare her love for him. "Hi," she said quietly.

He bent to kiss her cheek and whispered, "I hope it is truly alright to be here?"

"You are very welcome, Xavier," Kathleen answered his question. "We are sorry that Paris didn't answer you immediately. I had taken her out for a bite to eat as she was moping around the house all morning."

"Mum," Paris groaned, mortified that her mother had divulged that information.

Mick, Paris's short and stout father, stuck out his hands. "It is good to meet you, Xavier. Let me get your bag for you."

"Mr. and Mrs. Brendel, thank you for having me on such short notice. I can stay at a hotel if it is more convenient?"

"It's Kathleen and Mick, and no you won't be staying anywhere but here. You are Paris's boyfriend and you need to be shown some proper country hospitality."

Paris laughed nervously at her Mum calling Xavier her boyfriend. Could it get any more uncomfortable? At that moment she realized she had spoken too soon. Her two brothers barged their way out the house and down the stairs to present themselves to "the enemy," as they had been jokingly referring to Xavier since Paris had returned home this afternoon. Brooklyn, the eldest of the two boys and two years younger than Paris introduced himself, before the youngest sibling, Kent, quietly introduced himself. Kent was twenty, just as loud and brash as his siblings, but being gay in a country town, where many people still held backward opinions and saw it as something wrong, always made him wary of new people.

Xavier smiled and greeted them both warmly before moving to the boot to get his suitcase for Paris's waiting father. "Kent has volunteered his room for you to stay in and he will bunk in with Brooklyn," Mick explained.

"Oh, I don't want to kick anyone out of their bed. I am happy to bunk in the barn. Paris tells me it gets a workout over Christmas."

"It will be too hot to sleep in the barn tonight," Brooklyn

answered. "I don't mind. Kent doesn't snore too much and I am not sure if you snore or not as Paris hasn't told us, so you get your own room." Brooklyn laughed as his parents and Paris all said his name with varying degrees of exasperation.

"Sorry," Paris apologized as she tried to get her blushing under control. "Brooklyn thinks he is friggin' hilarious."

"I most certainly am freakin' hysterical. Now, you two have five minutes to get all lovey-dovey and ten minutes to change then we are leaving."

"Where are we going?" Paris asked. It was the first time she had been told that they would be going anywhere.

"Kent and I decided it is just too hot to not spend a few hours at the water hole before dinner. And I am sure The Enemy would agree." Brooklyn grinned as he used the new nickname.

Paris glowered at him, but her father got in first. "You have been raised with better manners than that, now apologize for making Paris's guest feel uncomfortable and behave yourself."

Brooklyn's heavy featured face showed that he understood that he may have let the teasing get out of hand, without giving Xavier a chance to understand it was all in jest. "Shit, sorry Xavier, I tend to have to watch myself at work all the time so when with family and friends I can be a little too much and push it."

Xavier smiled. "Really, it is no problem. The Enemy, huh?"

"Well, just for now. Let's see how you treat our sister." It was Kent who answered, to the surprise of everyone.

Paris groaned loudly enough for everyone to laugh. "Can everyone please give us a minute? Any more threats or stupid nicknames and he might just get in his car and leave."

"Are you coming to the waterhole?" Brooklyn asked as he did what they were told and began to move toward the front door.

Paris looked to Xavier, she wouldn't mind seeing him in a bathing suit again, but that also meant he would have to see her in hers. "Would you like to go swimming?"

"Sounds fun."

"Great, we will meet you on the porch in fifteen minutes," Brooklyn ordered before disappearing into the house behind his family.

Paris turned back to face Xavier to discover him standing close to her. He cupped her face in his hands and bent down to give her a slow lingering kiss. "I have been thinking about doing that all day." He let her face go and pulled her into a tight embrace.

She felt instantly at peace as she wrapped her arms around his waist and laid her head against his navy polo shirt. He had his usual gorgeous scent and her core burned as she thought of him naked. God, she couldn't believe how horny she was. "I can't believe you are here."

"We need to talk about a few things and I didn't want to wait and I wanted to do it face to face." Paris tensed at the words. Xavier kissed the top of her head and smoothed her hair as he liked to do. "Nothing bad. I just wanted to clear a few things up."

"I think that is a good idea."

He gave her a squeeze. "I can't wait to see you in your bathing suit again."

This made her giggle. "We'd best get going or my brother will drag us down ready or not."

Xavier let her go but took her hand. "Lead the way."

It didn't take Paris long to dig a pair of bathers she kept in her room for when she came home. They were bright red with large black roses and had a flared skirt and flattering rounded low back. She was quick in changing—throwing on a t-shirt and shorts, she put on a pair of old flip flops and grabbed two towels from the closet on her way back downstairs.

Brooklyn and Kent were already on the porch steps, one of them had brought around the flatbed Ute that they all used to get around the farm and parked next to Xavier's car. Her brothers were talking quietly as she approached, admiring the European expensive convertible. "I need to speak to you two quickly," Paris said in a low voice, checking to make sure Xavier wasn't coming.

Kent bent his head low to hers. "Love a good conspiracy, what you got?" he joked.

She didn't have time for their quips. "If Xavier decides to take his shirt off I don't need either of you guys commenting on his back."

Brooklyn raised his eyebrows at her. "Why would we?"

"He has a large birthmark on his back," she told them.

"Seriously?"

"Yes, seriously," she growled.

"No." Brooklyn gave her a funny look and Kent tsked at her. "Do you seriously think we would make fun of someone for something like that?"

Both her brothers stared at her and she had the grace to blush. "I didn't mean..." she tried to explain.

"Oh, but you did," Kent said quietly. "We are not all judgmental assholes."

"Ready?" asked Xavier as he opened the door. Stopping any further conversation.

Xavier

The dirt road was bumpy and Xavier was beginning to regret his choice to sit in the flat tray as his bones rattled and teeth chattered. It had seemed like a marvelous idea when Brooklyn had offered the choice that either Paris and Xavier sit in the cab, with Paris driving or they could sit in the back tray and experience something new. Xavier had asked Paris what she preferred, but she seemed preoccupied and had answered that either was fine with her. The late afternoon sun beat down on them and the metal from the tray was hot to touch everywhere but where they sat on a blanket. It was the height of summer and everything had dried out, increasing the dust as they trundled down the ancient road. They were moving too slowly to create enough breeze to aid them in cooling in any way. Xavier bit his lip, but what he really wanted to do was ask how much longer; though, knew he might get teased for sounding like a child if the brothers heard. He had tried to engage Paris in conversation twice, but she was unusually quiet and just squeezed his hand and answered quickly.

They had driven from the house back down the main driveway for about five hundred meters before turning off between two large trees onto a small dirt road that Xavier hadn't noticed on his way in. The trees thinned out for about ten minutes but then more plants and trees appeared, all far more lush green than anywhere else he had seen on the property so far. A few moments later and they came to stop in a small clearing. It was idyllic. With a slow-moving creek opening into a large oblongish shape for a hundred meters before thinning back down and disappearing around a corner. A gigantic eucalyptus tree sat close to the edge, many of its twisted impressive roots exposed. A large branch that reached out over the water held a thick rope with a huge knot tied at the bottom. Another branch on the opposite side held a makeshift swing. Paris's family had noticeably spent many hours down there as there was a large wooden table built with tree stumps for chairs and a fire pit surrounded by large river rocks.

The brothers grabbed the towels and an esky out of the tray without chatting and headed to the table. Xavier frowned but refrained from saying anything as he clambered out of the tray and helped the much shorter Paris down. Without waiting, the boys dumped the towels on the table, peeled off their t-shirts, and moved to the huge tree. Brooklyn was heavier than Kent, but both were powerfully built. Xavier watched with fascination as Kent grabbed hold of the thick knotted rope and pulled himself up until his feet rested on the knot and he half squatted. Brooklyn grabbed his brother around the waist and pulled him backward, slowly walking the both of them closer to the tree truck. "Ready?" Xavier heard Brooklyn ask.

"Hell, yeah," was the brash answer.

Without further warning, Brooklyn let go and Kent swung forward, out over the widened section of the large creek. With practiced grace, Kent let go of the rope at the peak of its arc and pushed with his powerful legs to jump off the knot and swan dive into the center of the water. He landed with a large splash that interrupted the tranquility of the surroundings and set the native birds to squawking.

Brooklyn whooped at the display. "Get out the way," he warned his brother.

Xavier continued to watch as Brooklyn took hold of the rope with one hand, but not quite as high as Kent had, and walked backward until he couldn't keep hold of the rope and continue to move. He grunted as he jumped up and hauled himself as high as he could and his feet found the knot. As he hadn't had the extra help of someone pulling him backward he didn't reach quite the height of Kent, but nonetheless still made an impressive splash as he let go of the rope and tucked up to bomb his nearby brother. Both laughed as he resurfaced.

"Would you like to try?" Paris asked as she gestured to the rope.

"Will you be doing it?" He was not sure why he had asked that. It was certainly out of his comfort zone, but maybe if she didn't do it he would be able to decline to not make her feel bad? His mother had been overprotective and his nature of not pushing boundaries had kept him from taking risks and doing things that he could not control the outcome.

"Absolutely," Paris grinned. "I told you I liked to swim in the family creek, it's why you took me to the beach, remember?"

"Yes, I just didn't know you liked to jump off swinging objects over questionably dangerous depths of water holes."

Paris smirked at Xavier and then her expression changed to one of concern. She moved closer to him and spoke quietly. "You don't have to do anything you don't want to. I can say I am not feeling it and then you can say you will just swim with me to keep me company."

Xavier blinked at her several times as he considered her words. If it had been the other way around he would have told her that while she was wonderful he wanted her to face her fears and not miss out. Like swimming at the beach. He had pushed her to leave her comfort zone, while here she was attempting to make him feel comfortable and safe. Maybe he should try to do a little more of that. Just listening to her and giving her the space and support to choose for herself.

"Come on, love birds, your turn," Brooklyn spoke loudly as he came out of the water, shaking his head and spraying water everywhere.

Xavier looked down at Paris and she smiled encouragingly. His heart beat a little faster as her hazel eyes sparkled with unspoken support. She was mesmerizing at this moment and he would much rather drag her off into the bush and have his way with her but that was not possible. His fingers itched to drag her bathing suit straps slowly down her shoulders and pull out her full, heavy breasts. Taking a deep breath and control of himself before his erection grew to a point no one would be able to ignore, Xavier decided that if he asked her to push her boundaries and accept herself then he needed to push his and try new things that were scary because he couldn't determine the outcome. "Okay, any tips for me?" He kissed Paris and let her go before turning to her brothers.

They both grinned and started giving him their own secret tips on how to get maximum splash and when to let go. Whether to stand up completely on the knot or squat to get a better arc like Kent had. They both assured him that the water was deep enough that he would not touch the bottom. Paris followed behind.

As they arrived at the rope Brooklyn frowned at him. "What?" Xavier asked.

"That fancy rash vest may get ruined by the friction with the rope. You sure you want to wear it?"

"Hadn't thought of that," admitted Xavier as he looked down at the navy short-sleeved vest with its white logo and stripes along the shoulders.

"No one gives a shit about your birthmark, if that makes you feel better," Kent spoke quietly.

Xavier was surprised at the mention of his birthmark and he looked to Paris to find her glaring at her brother. "I don't care if you see my birthmark. I learned to accept it years ago. It is more about exposing it to something that may irritate it. I find sand to be a hassle," he explained.

"No sand here, so you should be fine." Brooklyn looked to Paris. "So, not his hang up, but yours. You now projecting it onto others?"

Xavier didn't know what was going on but Paris looked upset and he wanted to protect her. "Paris, it was thoughtful of you to try to protect my feelings, but I get the feeling your brothers aren't the type to make fun of me for that, even though I am the enemy." He turned to her brothers. "And I am positive over the years you have given her a hard time and hurt her feelings often enough that she couldn't completely be sure you would behave because it would be fun to annoy her."

All three looked a little shamed-faced. Now he needed to sound not so pompous and bring it all back to a level where they could joke and tease each other. The only way to do that was to admit his fear. "Okay, now I am not as adventurous as Paris so this rope swing scares me, but I want to give it a go." He pulled his swimming vest off over his head. "Let's do this."

Kent gasped as he looked at Xavier's exposed back. Xavier was amazed that after the discussion they had had that he had reacted that way.

"Kent," Paris hissed.

Paris's youngest brother began to laugh. "You have the most perfect back muscles I have ever seen." Xavier turned with his eyebrows raised; it was not the response he had expected. "And now I can see the front you are built like a mythological God. I only have one question."

Brooklyn and Paris groaned.

"What?" asked Xavier.

"You don't happen to have a gay brother or cousin, who shares your same stunning qualities?" Kent winked at him.

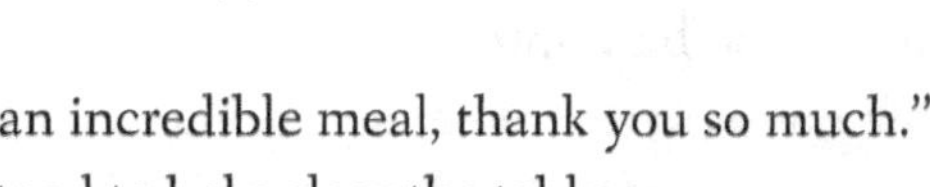

"*T*hat was an incredible meal, thank you so much." Xavier stood to help clear the table.

"What are you doing?" asked Kathleen.

"Helping clear the dishes, like the others are doing." Xavier frowned. Had he done something wrong?

"Guests don't do dishes. That is the kids' job, irrelevant

of how old they are. They only get out of the chore when they have children old enough to do the task for them," Mick explained.

"I really don't mind," Xavier attempted to assure them.

"No, Kathleen and I want to get to know you better. Come sit with us on the porch."

Paris smiled and took the plates from Xavier's hands. "It's fine, go sit with Mum and Dad."

Mick picked up his drink and headed through the family room and out the back screen door, and Xavier followed suit. He hadn't been on the back porch yet and was awestruck with the landscape that greeted him. The vista was magnificent. Flat grassland flecked with fluffy white sheep expanded out before them. A single tall windmill stood slowly spinning some distance away and something reflected beneath it, Xavier guessed it was the dam that the creek fed into and that kept the sheep watered. Fence posts spotted the fields and the odd tree sat baking in the harsh sun. The flat grassland eventually became gently rolling hills covered with denser growing trees.

"You have an amazing home. Paris was lucky to grow up here," Xavier spoke as he looked out upon the peaceful view.

"Thank you." Mick settled into a large wicker chair that looked out onto the horizon, while Kathleen sat in a second identical chair, a small matching table in between the two chairs was where they placed their drinks. This was clearly where they spent their evenings. A two-seater wicker lounge with rooster decorated cushions sat on a right angle to the chairs, but still allowed room for people to move by on the large verandah. Xavier took a seat on the lounge and sipped his drink. He was nervous but determined to make a good impression on Paris's parents.

"Why Paris?" Mick asked.

Xavier was startled by the direct question. "Sorry?" He stalled by making him repeat it.

"We don't have a lot of time alone. The kids will be back out soon and we could fill the passing minutes with chit chat or you can tell me why Paris. She is smitten with you and your charms, I want to know why you are smitten with my girl?"

Xavier thought back to his conversation with his mother and that once he had spoken from the heart she had respected him and what he wanted. Perhaps if he did the same here and showed his vulnerability, it would be the quickest way for her parents to understand how important Paris had become to him. "She is brilliant, capable, funny, and kind. Her enthusiasm is contagious and I love her zest for life. She lights up a room and can ease other's worries." He paused and smiled to himself for a moment. "Her confidence in her abilities is attractive, I admire that she knows her worth in her workplace and demands their respect. The few friends of hers that I have met are very much in awe of her, and she exudes cheerfulness." Xavier stopped and looked at Mick and Kathleen, he could talk about Paris all day and all of her amazing qualities and why he loved her.

It was Mick who spoke first. "My daughter is all of those things and I am grateful that she has found someone who can see she is as special as we believe she is. But Paris is not perfect and you can't make her perfect. She has faults and some she needs help to overcome and some she needs to be loved despite. The trick is to know the difference."

"Have you told her you love her?" Kathleen was more forward with her words.

Strangely the question didn't frighten him. "No."

"But you do?"

He looked at Paris's mother and tried to make his face look as sincere as he felt. "I have never loved anyone like I love Paris. It has only been a few short weeks, but I want to be with her forever, with your permission." He looked to Mick.

"Are you asking what I think you are asking?" Mick asked softly.

Xavier checked the windows to see if any of the siblings were lurking, rather than in the kitchen doing their chores. The family area was empty. "I am not exactly sure what I am asking. But if the topic came up at some point I would like to know that you are okay with the idea."

Both of her parents looked at him without speaking for quite some time and he was growing uncomfortable. Perhaps he had misjudged the situation and should have remained silent? After all, he didn't even know if Paris felt the same way, and now he had exposed himself to people who were essentially strangers. All of a sudden he felt incredibly vulnerable, but also amazed at his willingness to be open about his emotions for the first time, though he had yet to be with the one person they were about.

"Yes."

Mick's word interrupted his panicking thoughts.

"If there comes a point and you want to ask then ask without fear of our interference. You obviously love our daughter but you also have sincere respect for who she is and that is a rare thing to find." Paris's father stood and shook his hand.

"Don't I get a say in this?" Kathleen also stood.

"Mrs. Brendel, of course you do." Xavier was quick to assure her.

"Xavier, it's Kathleen, and that question was aimed at my husband, not you."

"Oh."

"Sorry, Kath, I got a bit carried away. You know how I get."

Xavier raised his eyebrows at the comment.

The short man turned back to him. "I am a hopeless romantic. Kath is the far more practical one, but it is a well-kept secret so I don't get ribbed by my buddies and kids."

"We already know, Dad. We think it is kind of sweet so never said anything." Paris pushed open the screen door, carrying a drying cloth and a sweet smile for her father. "Why were you talking about romance?" she asked as she hung the towel across the railing.

"Xavier asked if he could borrow the ute tomorrow night so you two could go out and have a picnic for dinner and look at the stars. I was just suggesting that out near the dam would be the perfect place to get away from all the lights to see the sky and its star systems without interference."

Xavier was impressed by Mick's smooth cover-up and it was also an excellent idea. "I thought we could go into town tomorrow and you can show me around and we can pick up some food for the picnic?" He went with it.

Paris's eyes lit up and she went and hugged her father. "That is a wonderful plan, thanks, Dad."

Mick returned his daughter's hug. "Anything to make my daughter happy." He smiled at Xavier over Paris's head.

"Yes," Kathleen agreed, and she smiled at Xavier encouragingly. "Though completely unexpected, I think it is a wonderful idea."

Xavier got the distinct impression that Kathleen was not talking about the picnic. Now he had to find the courage to tell Paris just how much she meant to him. He was still slightly in awe of his emotions and how rapidly they had developed for the potty-mouthed, vivacious woman with her heavenly curves.

CHAPTER TWELVE
PARIS

The feeling of Xavier's hand in hers was comforting and thrilling and Paris wanted to continually squeeze his hand to reassure herself that this was real. They had parked his convertible in her father's mechanic shop's driveway that sat on the end of the main street in town. It was difficult to find a parking spot as the street was flooded with locals picking up final items for Australia Day barbeque preparations for the next day, and tourists taking advantage of the gorgeous mild summer day to explore the area.

"What are you going to show me first?" he asked.

"I was thinking we would just walk up and down the main street. The supermarket is down this end so we can pick up supplies for the picnic tonight on the way back. Everything that happens here pretty much happens along this strip."

"Lead the way."

Paris chose the side opposite the supermarket so they would go by it on their way back when they walked down the side of the road. Paris had never held hands and walked with a guy she cared about before, and she found the experience something she wanted to repeat, often. Xavier squeezed her hand causing her to look up at him and return the soft smile he gave her. They walked by packed cafes and antique shops; the local hippie shop with its crystals, tarot cards, and woven hemp handbags appeared to be popular. They reached the middle of their side and the buildings ceased and were replaced by large parkland. Paris always loved that moment of transition from the hustle and bustle of businesses trading to the tranquility of the lush green grass and large weeping willows that filled the area. Rather than continue to walk along the straight footpath on the side of the road, she chose the one that wound its way deeper into the park and split itself into several different choices to enjoy the area.

"This is beautiful. Did you spend much time here growing up?"

"Not as much as many locals. With my brothers at home and the creek and all that open space, we didn't need to come into town to play. Though I did use to hang out here a lot in my early high school years. You know some great places to hide to sneak a cigarette and fantasize about boys with your bestie," she spoke the words lightly, fighting the hidden pain those memories caused.

They walked by laughing children playing on the large, well-appointed playground that her mother had helped fundraise for two years prior. The park was busier than normal as it was early afternoon and the park provided plenty of places to sit in the shade and picnic. A football bounced across their path and Paris let go of Xavier's hand to bend down and pick it up. She searched for the owner of the ball and found a young girl and her father waving from a short distance away. Paris kicked the ball to them and it landed squarely on the man's chest

Xavier whistled. "Nice kick."

"Thanks." She retook his hand. "With two brothers and a dad who loves AFL, if I wanted to be included I figured I better learn how to kick a footy. How are your footy-kicking skills?"

"I was the stereotypical Asian boy you see on TV. A maths geek, with a Tiger mum who had little time for sports and girls. I was also quite skinny, so the thought of being pummeled by all those huge football players was a tad daunting." He puffed out his defined chest and looked down at her. "Though, I now have the physique I sadly do not have the matching skill set."

Paris laughed. "That's easily fixed. I can teach you, as long as you don't mind learning from a girl?"

They had walked into a quieter area of the park and Xavier pulled her behind a large tree. He pressed her against the ancient trunk and lowered his lips to hers. Paris responded instantly, opening her mouth, her tongue joining his. She reached up and curled her fingers in his short, dark hair, while her other hand moved to his back and found its way under his shirt, to find his soft, hot skin. As she lightly trailed her hand across the band of his pants he moaned softly in response. She deepened the kiss and tightened her fingers, gently tugging his hair. For a few short seconds, all thoughts of propriety left her and she could think of nothing more than fucking him here against the tree. Fortunately, the voices of children singing nearby brought her back to her senses and she pushed him slightly away from her, panting with the effort it took to control herself.

His eyes were slightly glazed as he rested his forehead on hers. "You can teach me anything you want. I happen to think you are amazing." He kissed the tip of her nose before disentangling himself from her and adjusting the beginnings of his erection.

"I think you're amazing too." She spoke the words hesitantly. It was still difficult for her to be open about her feelings.

He retook her hand and lifted it to his mouth, kissing each knuckle. "You might want to steer me out of this park, my gentlemanly ways may not last much longer if I am left alone with you." He softly kissed the inside of her wrist, which set her pulse racing again. "I crave you, Paris. In every way."

"Fuck me," she breathed.

He raised an eyebrow at her. "Is that an invitation?"

"Holy hell, if we weren't in a park in the middle of the day with lots of kids around, you would be in so much trouble." Paris smiled cheekily at him, knowing he was too much of a gentleman to do anything more than talk about it.

"So, let's get the tour of the town back on track then."

He pulled her out from behind the tree and they proceeded down the winding path as if nothing had happened. Though now Paris's mind kept wandering to what it would have been like to be taken up against that tree. *Focus, Paris,* she chided to herself.

After a few minutes of walking, they came upon a pretty wooden bridge that allowed you to cross over the wide stream that ran through the park. A few children were feeding a mother duck and her baby ducklings by the edge of the slow running water, while further along a group of teenagers were shrieking as they splashed water at each other. Several old men stood at the center of the bridge, attempting to catch fish while frowning at everyone who disturbed the water. Paris had no clue why they bothered to fish there when there were more bridges in the park that would make better and quieter fishing spots. Several pre-teen boys rode their bikes over the bridge, earning themselves dirty looks from the men. Paris smiled at their grumpiness.

"We won't cross this time. Over the other side behind that row of trees are the town's soccer ground, outdoor netball courts, and BMX track. The footy oval, cricket pitch, as well as the basketball and netball stadium are part of the high school."

Xavier looked impressed as they walked back up towards the road. "I didn't realize your town was so big. What a great place to grow up."

Paris shrugged. "Anywhere is a good place to grow up if you are good at sport or are attractive."

Xavier squeezed her hand but didn't contradict her. "It sometimes takes us a while to find our place and people."

They walked out of the park and back into the busy main street. Paris put her arm out and pointed in the general direction down the road. "So, further down, on both sides is mostly businesses; real estate, lawyers, doctors, dentists, police station, CFA, with the odd cafe thrown in for them to have meetings and eat lunch. At the end of the business is both the primary and secondary school on one side and the other is the gallery, local museum, and theatre, where all productions are held. My favorite bakery is next to the theatre, they do the best chocolate eclairs in Victoria." She turned him toward the opposite side of the road. "And here is the local pub. No self-respecting Australian country town does not boast a pub where you can get a parma and chips for a minimal amount of money."

Xavier laughed at this statement. "Mmmm... really?"

Paris looked shocked. "You have traveled the world but don't know that every pub in Australia offers a parma and chips at a reasonable price and they all claim theirs is the best?"

Xavier looked sheepish. "What can I say?"

"I think we need to rectify this now. How do you feel about sharing food?"

"I would share anything with you."

Paris's heart sang for a moment at the admission. "Well, let's get your cute butt over there and you can try the best parma and chips in Australia right now. I was thinking we might share one, as they are huge and I don't want to spoil our picnic?"

"Sounds perfect to me."

The pair crossed the road and found a place in the old pub, with its worn wooden fixtures and friendly atmosphere. They managed to find a small table on the balcony of the second floor that overlooked the street and all its comings and goings. As Paris settled into her chair she had a moment of complete happiness. It looked like her life was finally the way she wished it would be.

"I have to use the bathroom so I will order. Would you like a drink?" the most handsome man in the place asked her.

"There is usually a deal. A pot and parma for a certain price. Just get us that," she explained, managing to not roll her eyes at someone that could have lived in Australia for so long but didn't know that.

Xavier hesitated a moment further and she laughed, realizing his dilemma. "A pot of any of the beers that are on tap will be fine."

"Great, no problem."

Paris looked out onto the street of her hometown and saw it from Xavier's perspective rather than her own and she could see its appeal. The beautiful park, filled with fun and families opposite, the quaint shops and quirky ones that lined the street. The way that most people greeted you as you walked by them and the sense of an easy-going pace. Even the hustle and bustle of tourists couldn't label the town anything but sedate. The city was where she thrived, but she could completely understand why her parents and brothers chose to stay here.

"Oh my, look who is back in town. Gracing us with her presence," a female voice dripping with sarcasm interrupted her peace.

Paris closed her eyes in an attempt to block out the nasty voice behind her. She didn't turn or respond.

"I am surprised they let her sit out on the balcony," a male voice joined in, his voice filled with feigned surprise. "Is it sturdy enough?" His implications were clear.

Paris continued to look out on the street, refusing to rise to the bait of her high school tormentors, Tracey and Jack.

"Look at her, thinking she is better than us. All haughty 'cause she is a big city girl now." Tracey's voice was needling.

Paris jumped as Jack's voice whispered in her ear, "Big is right. You still make me heave when I look at you as if I would ever find you attractive."

She didn't turn, but she did find her voice. Something she had not done before. "Jack, I think you are vile," her voice shook, but she spoke anyway. "Would you two please get a life and leave me alone?" With those final words, she gathered her courage and turned to face her high school bullies.

The perfect country town couple stood before her. Jack, his arms crossed over his sculptured chest wore Blundstone boots, torn faded jeans, a muscle shirt, and a taunting sneer across his handsome face. Tracey, his perfect counterpart, wore tiny denim shorts, her blonde hair in cute pigtails, a mid-drift top to show her tanned flat stomach, and a look of contempt on her pretty face.

Paris felt ill; they had her cornered. Typically, if she saw them she hid, and on the rare occasion they managed to get close enough to talk to her, she was usually able to walk away without enduring their taunting for more than a few words. Unless she made a scene to get them to move out of her way, she would have to sit and take their spiteful words. She doubted her desire for them to leave her alone was going to be enough to make them leave.

She was right.

"Oh, no, have we upset the precious princess?" Tracey giggled.

"Just like the old days, huh, Paris?" Jack's smile was full of venom and she braced herself for his next words. "You sitting all by yourself. No one wanting to be your friend. Poor big, Paris." He sniggered.

Tears stung the back of her eyes as she fought for control. She abruptly stood, needing to get out of there.

"I think you two should apologize and leave," a voice spoke behind them.

Paris's worlds collided and she bowed her head in shame.

Xavier

Xavier caught the last words the guy who stood in front of Paris said as he approached carrying their drinks.

"You sitting all by yourself. No one wanting to be your friend. Poor big, Paris." He had snickered.

An unexpected need to protect Paris and hurt this person viscerally permeated Xavier's soul and it took all of his self-control to not drop the glasses he carried to punch the guy in the face. Whoever he was looked strong, but Xavier knew he was stronger. Keeping a tight rein on his anger he spoke forcefully. "I think you two should apologize and leave."

As they both turned to confront him, Xavier saw the panic and humiliation on Paris's face. Her cheeks were red and her beautiful hazel eyes were full of unshed tears. His heart constricted and his jaw tightened as he watched her hide her face.

The young woman who would have been pretty in a conventional way except for the sneer plastered on her face spoke, her head lifted in challenge. "We ain't doing nothing that concerns you."

"Anything to do with Paris concerns me," Xavier spoke firmly.

The ruggedly handsome cowboy looked him up and down as if judging who would win in a fight. Xavier noted his body relax slightly as if he could sense Xavier didn't want trouble, just for them to leave Paris alone. "We are just old friends catching up, right, Paris?"

"Who are you?" the girl asked, hands on hips, looking as if she was used to getting her own way.

"I am Paris's boyfriend and I expect you to leave her alone from now on." Xavier looked the guy in the eye. "Do we understand each other?"

Xavier prayed that they would walk away. He had never been in a fight and had no desire to ever hit someone, but if this jerk hurt Paris further he would do what needed to be done to protect her. He noted Paris had finally lifted her head and was staring at him in wonder. His heart broke for her. What had these horrid people done to her?

"Yeah," the guy answered. "No need to get all worked up."

Xavier moved to the side to allow him to move.

"Come on, Trace. Let's not stand around with these losers."

Xavier chose to ignore the taunt. The guy was a bully with a chip on his shoulder. The pretty girl looked up at him and fluttered her lashes, which he assumed got her all sorts of things from men. "You would prefer that over this?" she purred softly, no one but Xavier and Paris able to hear her.

"Paris does things for me that you never could, you pale in comparison," he answered.

"Asshole," Tracey hissed as she moved away.

Xavier turned to face Paris, all thoughts of the bullies forgotten as he looked at her sad, beautiful face. He pulled her in for a hug; she was stiff against his body, but she slowly began to relax as he stroked her hair. He opened his mouth to tell her how he felt, that he loved her. This would be the perfect time as she needed to know that she was special but his moment was interrupted by the waiter with their chicken parmigiana and chips.

CHAPTER THIRTEEN
XAVIER

Xavier sat back in his camp chair and watched the orange sun sink further toward the horizon. He reached out and put his hand on Paris's thigh as she sat close next to him in her camp chair. They sat in silence as they watched the sun slowly inch its way from the sky. They had had a wonderful picnic, though it was a little subdued compared to their afternoon walk and Xavier knew it had something to do with the two people he had found harassing Paris. She had not said anything about the encounter, but he knew that it was playing on her mind.

"Paris," Xavier began just as Paris spoke.

"Xavier," she said at the same time.

He let her go first in the hope she would tell him what was bothering her.

"I was wondering how you feel about exerting a little energy?" she raised her eyebrows suggestively at him. "We have about half an hour before it will be too dark."

"Too dark for what?" he asked.

"For what I have in mind."

"I am intrigued."

"Great." Paris stood and moved to the back of the ute. Xavier stood and followed. What was she doing?

With a triumphant grin, Paris took an AFL football from her large bag and held it out to him. "Let's teach you to kick this sucker properly, so my brothers have one less thing to tease you about."

Xavier laughed as he took the oval-shaped ball. "Deal."

Paris was a patient teacher as she showed him where to put his hands and how to line up the laces. It was good to see her relax and laugh again even if it was at his expense. By the time the sun was casting shadows too long for them to see, his foot ached, but his heart sang.

He sat and poured a glass of wine for each of them as he watched Paris light the fire she had prepared earlier, in the fire pit that was a permanent fixture near the dam. The large car was parked between them and the main house so even if her brothers felt the need to pry they wouldn't be able to see anything. His eyes wandered to her gorgeous arse as she bent to tend the fire. "I admire how capable you are out here."

Paris stood and looked at him. "What do you mean?"

"You build fires and swing from ropes to jump into the water. You are impressive."

"I am a coward and a fraud."

Her words were so soft that he almost missed them.

Xavier stood and moved to her. "No, no. You are wrong." He pulled her down onto the picnic blanket that they had not packed up yet. "Don't talk like that."

"It's true." Paris sat down next to him. "I put on this big act, but when confronted I can't defend myself."

"I disagree." He turned to face her. "You're pretty good at confronting me when you feel slighted."

She smiled weakly at him. "Honestly, that is more of a defense mechanism than anything else. I jump at you rather than deal with why I feel that way or letting you in."

"Oh, but I think I deserved your wrath when I asked you to tone down the swearing." He reached up and touched her face, running his thumb along her smooth cheek. "Sometimes I am an idiot." He leaned in and kissed her. "Talk to me. Tell me who they were."

"They are the reason I have difficulty trusting anyone."

A tear slid down her face and he wiped it away. "You are safe."

"Tracey was once my best friend. We did everything together. Dance class, netball, skipping school, talking boys, we were always together. She holds all my schoolgirl secrets and the biggest one was that I was madly in love with Jack. He had been kind to me once in primary school, sharing his lunch when I had left mine at home." Her voice trembled as the words spilled out.

Xavier continued to stroke her face, offering her comfort, but he didn't speak in the hope she would continue to confide in him. He kept his own emotions in check; he would have time to tell her exactly what he thought of the two bullies once her story was told.

"As we started high school it became clear that Jack was going to be one of those guys. Popular, sporty, and handsome—a lethal combination that can be amazing in the right guy and hideous in the wrong guy. He turned into the wrong type. Jack soon learned that if he was cruel, but in a funny way, the kids would laugh with him and he could get away with his taunting and snide remarks." Paris gave a bitter laugh. "Tracey and I would talk about how sweet and kind Jack used to be and if we were together I could show him how to be good again. How fucking crazy is that?" Paris looked at him, her hazel eyes vulnerable. "Anyway, the years went on and he pretty much left me alone, ignoring my existence. But everything changed when he and Tracey landed the lead roles in the school production and fell in love."

Paris began to cry, and Xavier did the only thing he could—he held her. He made soothing noises and rubbed her back, wishing he could say something to take her pain away.

Through her sobs, she continued. "I can't believe it still affects me this much. Tracey didn't have the guts to tell me to my face that she was going out with my once-secret crush; instead, she walked right by me at lunchtime and sat with him and his friends, ignoring me completely." She sniffed loudly and wiped her nose with the edge of her flannel shirt. "From that day we were no longer friends and we have never talked about her betrayal." Her crying calmed and she snuggled into his shoulder, burying her face in his chest. "You know, I would have been able to handle them being together if they didn't both turn cruel. I could have been both of their friends, but instead of Tracey bringing out his kindness, Jack brought out her bitchiness. And then she did what no friend should do." Paris stopped and the unspoken treachery hung there.

"Tracey told Jack that you had had a crush on him?" Xavier guessed.

"Yes," muttered Paris. "He confronted me in the middle

of the schoolyard, with everyone around." Her voice was so faint Xavier had to strain to hear it over the crackling of the fire. "Jack laughed and told me that I was hideous and that he would never go out with someone so fat and ugly. He said I was disgusting and no one would want me. Tracey stood beside him, pretty and thin and nodding as if she agreed with everything he said. No one stood up for me, as they all feared being Jack's next target."

Xavier continued to calmly rub his palm in circles on the small of her back. He was furious and heartbroken for what she had experienced. "Please tell me they left you alone after that?"

"I endured several weeks of them teasing me until someone told my brothers what was happening, and though they were younger they had many friends who were willing to let me sit with them at lunch break. They were kind, but I was lonely and it seemed that every time I was by myself Tracey and Jack would find me and insult me. I couldn't wait to get out of here once I had finished school. I reinvented myself and became loud, brash, and tough, but when I come home I am terrified of running into them as I slip back into that victim role so easily and I let them attack me." The tears had completely dried as she raised her face to his. "I don't let people in, I don't share my secrets because I don't want them thrown back at me. I have lots of friends, but none that know me well because it is so hard for me to trust that people are good."

Everything fell into place from the incident with her brothers at the rope swing yesterday. Xavier tucked a stray strand of auburn hair behind her ear. "That is why your brother told you that not everyone is an asshole and why you thought they might say something about my birthmark." Her eyes glittered in the firelight and he leaned toward her, his voice compassionate. "You can trust me."

"I want to trust you." Her voice caught, but she held his stare.

This was the moment he knew he needed to show her his vulnerability. Drop his guard and let her in. There was no use in ignoring his feelings for her any longer—it served no purpose. "Paris, I love you." The words were simple and he was amazed at how easily it had been to say them.

"Xavier," she spoke clearly, her face filled with wonder. "I want to love you."

He smiled, his heart happy. It was enough for now. After what she had divulged he had a better understanding of how brittle she was underneath the sassy exterior. "Thank you for trusting me with your secret. I have a secret I need to tell you now." He looked at her, his face serious and his anger simmering.

"Go on." Her eyes were wide as if she could sense his underlying ire.

"I have never wanted to pummel someone as much as I wanted to hit Jack." He let his breath and his anger subsided. "And I wouldn't mind giving Tracey a talking to about manners and friendship."

Paris began to giggle.

"What?" Xavier was shocked at the response.

"You are so freakin cute. I can just imagine you politely telling Tracey off and I wonder how you punch someone in a gentlemanly manner?"

Xavier narrowed his eyes at her. "You are making fun of me."

"Just a little." She reached up and cupped his chin with both hands. "Can you ever forgive me?" she teased.

His stomach fluttered and deeper within him the flames of desire grew. This was the Paris he knew, the one that made him long to be with her, inside her, exploring her. He reconciled the scared, traumatized Paris, afraid to trust with the flirty vixen who wanted to play. He loved both and all the other sides he was yet to uncover.

"Have you ever made love under the stars?" he asked, surprising himself with the question—it seemed she brought the naughty out of him.

Paris moved the hand that cupped his chin and rubbed her thumb across his lips. "Take your shirt off and we can discuss it."

It was Xavier's turn to chuckle, but he did what he was told and dragged his t-shirt over his head. Paris ran a finger down the center of his chest and he shivered in response, her barest touch made him hard. She continued down to the waist band of his shorts and continued on until she rubbed her hand over his hardness and squeezed him gently. Xavier's insides clenched and he licked his lips as he pushed Paris back onto the blanket. He moved until he lay on top of her, his legs resting inbetween hers, he pushed his hips down, rubbing himself against her as he lowered his head to kiss her.

Paris's lips parted and he felt her tongue seek his. The kiss was passionate and urgent, but he slowed it, wanting to express something other than lust. He rested on one elbow and moved so his hand could reach the small blue buttons on her cute floral dress. He deftly undid the buttons one-handed and slid his hand inside the soft fabric to find her ample breast. Xavier ran tiny kisses along her neck and down her collarbone before he came to the top of her bra, and then ran his tongue across to the other breast. He felt her nipple pressed firm against the lacy cup and gently pinched it, making Paris arch her back toward him. She was delicious.

While his fingers played with her nipple, his mouth bit the other one through the lace, the groan she let out was electrifying and he took it into his mouth and sucked harder. Paris fisted her hand into his hair and pulled it, Xavier was surprised at his body's response as he ground his hard on against her. He longed to be inside her. Her other hand moved over his back and when she reached his waistband she gave it a tug, clearly telling him what she wanted.

Xavier knelt back and looked at her, her dress undone to the waist and her beautiful breasts barely contained in a sexy black lacy bra. Her thick auburn hair darker in the moonlight spread out around her, shining with the firelight. She was mesmerising and perfect and he had to have her now. As he moved to take off his shorts and boxers, he watched Paris move her legs to one side and slide off her panties. She laid back down, and while she hadn't removed her dress she didn't bother to pull her top closed. It was definitely progress.

Paris reached her hands out to him, and he smiled at her as he lowered himself back on top of her, resting on his elbows. Her hands rested on his shoulders before they moved up to the back of his neck. She parted her legs and he leaned down to kiss her, his arms sliding down and under her shoulders. The tip of him came to rest against her, and as Xavier's tongue danced with Paris's, he pushed his hips forward and entered her. She raised her hips to meet him and bent her knees to allow him deeper access.

The warmth and wetness of her surrounded him and Xavier groaned as she encased him completely—they were the perfect fit. He pulled back until his tip rested just inside her before pushing back in, again and again, lovingly, gently. With each thrust, her hips tilted to bring them together. Xavier covered Paris in light kisses; her neck, her ears, the soft spot under her ear lobes, the corners of her mouth, and the tip of her nose. As his orgasm built, he controlled his movements, allowing her to build with him, making sure he was aware of her little signs that she had found the right position to create the right type of friction. The delay was exquisite and his core tightened further to barely containable need.

Paris whimpered softly and Xavier had by now learned that was her tell tale sign and he thrust deep and hard several times as they both toppled over the edge of bliss. He watched her hazel eyes widen as she stilled beneath him before arching her back and shuddering silently. Xavier dropped his head to rest against her forehead as he was carried away with the sensation of her muscles contracting around him, his own body shaking slightly with the aftermath. "I love you, Paris," he told her for the second time.

*D*on't forget to put your rubbish out. Xox

She pressed send and then put the phone down. Paris sang softly to herself as she settled in her desk chair and switched on her computer. It was Tuesday morning and life was wonderful. They had returned late last night from her parents' property, and even though they had spent the day together he had rung to make certain she had got home safely as they had taken separate cars because of his surprise visit. Paris had marveled at how easy it was to talk to him about anything and they had chatted for an hour before agreeing they should hang up as they both had work the following day.

Her phone vibrated and she jumped at it.

You are a lifesaver. Almost walked out without doing it. I would have returned to a very stinky apartment. See, this is why I love you. Xox

Paris blinked at the message. Her phone vibrated in her hand and she jumped.

You got time for lunch today?

It was her friend Mandi.

For you, yes. Meet you at 1 at the lifts?

Perfect. :-)

Paris held the phone in her hands a few moments longer as she tried to decide how to answer Xavier's text. Flirty, cute, funny... she could ponder this all day she realized, so, in the end, she went for sincere.

Have a safe flight. Ring me tonight when you get the chance. Xox

The morning went quickly as she organized last-minute details to help the foreign students settle in. Orientation would now be commencing for many schools and this was the time things typically fell apart and gaps in the system were exposed.

The reminder she had set herself went off and she hustled to the bathroom and then back to her desk to grab her bag and phone before she met Mandi at the elevators. "Hey, spunk," Mandi called out as Paris walked down the corridor. "Did you have a good long weekend? You sure look happier than what you sounded like when I talked you to last Thursday."

Paris reached Mandi and gave her a quick hug. "He turned up at my folk's place on Saturday."

"Well, fuck me," Mandi said a little too loudly, causing a few people to look their way and a middle-aged woman to frown at them over her black-rimmed glasses.

This made them both dissolve into hysterics as they

pushed each other into the lift like they were thirteen-year-olds on their first outing away from their parents. "How was your weekend?" Paris asked as the elevator began its journey to the lobby.

"David and I broke up." Mandi shook her platinum blonde bob and her gray eyes turned a shade of steel. "Turns out the bastard was seeing me and some other chick. She rang while he was in the shower. Set her straight and we both dumped him. What a prick, hey?"

The lift doors swished opened and Paris and Mandi quickly filed out. The reception area was busy so Paris waited until they left the building to stop and give Mandi a longer, heartfelt hug. "I am so sorry. Men can be such assholes."

"Not yours, it would appear."

Paris linked her arm through her friend's in a show of comradeship and they walked to the local Sushi Train. Once they were seated and had ordered a drink, Paris looked at Mandi. "Do you want to talk about it? I am here for the whole sordid rehash if needed." She looked at her seriously, all silliness gone.

Mandi shrugged her thin shoulders and tucked her hair behind her ear. "Nah. I might soon, but at the moment it is too raw and I want to think about something else. Can we change the subject?" She picked up her can of Fanta and sipped through the paper straw, making a face as she did so. Mandi had voiced her opinion on the demise of the plastic straw on several occasions.

"I have a subject we can discuss."

"Go on," Mandi urged.

Paris snagged a plate of tuna and avocado sushi as it

went by on the conveyor belt. "Do you think falling in love and knowing someone is your forever person within four weeks is truly possible?"

Mandi took a plate of salmon sashimi and took a bite before she answered the question. The girls' usual fun and loud conversations were replaced with real-life problems and decisions. "Actually, this might surprise you, but I do. I think it is possible but it rarely happens as people are too busy playing games and not being honest with themselves or the other person. Why?"

Paris finished her sushi and kept her eye out for an egg sushi roll to make its way around to her. "Xavier told me he loved me."

Mandi whooped and clapped her hands. "That is fuckin' huge."

They both sat and watched the sushi glide by on its cute little conveyor belt, eating silently for a moment.

"Paris, what did you say when he said he loved you?"

"I didn't return the sentiment, if that is what you are asking."

"You don't love him?" Mandi narrowed her gray eyes. "Or you don't want to love him because that is scary?"

Paris wanted to shrug. She was regretting starting the conversation. "I think he is my forever person, but if that is the case and I let him in, I am giving him the ability to destroy me."

"That is an odd way to look at it."

"Most people go through life trying to find a person who treats them well, returns their love, does it for them in the bedroom, and treats them as an equal... you find that person, and all you can think about is not wanting to be open because you might get hurt."

Paris was silent.

Mandi went on. "And this is coming from a woman who has just found out her boyfriend of five months had been cheating on her the whole time."

"I had a few shitty moments on my weekend if it helps you at all."

"What happened to you? We shall compare notes."

"Ran into my high school bullies who turned out to be just as nasty as ever, made Xavier and my brothers feel incredibly uncomfortable due to my insecurities, and then proceeded to cry all over Xavier on our romantic night camping."

Mandi's eyes widened for a moment and then she began to laugh. "Oh my God, Paris."

Paris began to laugh too. "What a pair we make."

"I think I still win the worst weekend title."

"How so?"

"Because you, you lucky bitch, got laid by the hottest guy out there."

Paris almost snorted rice everywhere.

"What I want to know is if have you played dress-up yet? After all, he has that very sexy pilot uniform..." Mandi wiggled her eyebrows at Paris.

"No, we haven't, but now you have mentioned it."

CHAPTER FIFTEEN
PARIS

The end of the week could not have come quick enough for Paris. She had missed Xavier more than she thought possible and had quickly concluded that she needed to be honest and tell him that she loved him and wanted to commit to him. It was a scary thought to finally be that honest with someone, but every time she had shown her vulnerability he had been there and supported her. Her frank discussion with Mandi had helped solidify her resolve and admit that though she wasn't playing games, she wasn't being honest with someone who was prepared to be honest with her. She wasn't sure if that was enough, his ideas were always elaborate, yet thoughtful. He had a way of showing her that he listened and wanted to please her.

To show how she felt, Paris thought she would surprise Xavier by going to his apartment and making him a romantic meal of his favorite Indian dish. When Paris had rung and spoken to May and Taree they had both encouraged her to do a less formal welcome home and declaration and maybe just arrive with champagne, chocolate-dipped strawberries, and Taree had added the suggestion of a sexy negligee. The last had made Paris blush and she was grateful they couldn't see her.

With every passing day, the urge to reply to his "love you" texts and conversation endings grew. Paris wanted to blurt it out, to yell it from the rooftops, and to tell anyone that she met that she, Paris Brendel, had found her forever person. The only thing stopping her was that she wanted to say it to his face, rather than over the phone or via text. It was too important to say flippantly.

Paris hummed to herself as she waited for the elevator to arrive. She checked her watch, she was half an hour early but she couldn't wait any longer—she needed to see Xavier. Her want and longing had grown and now she fully understood why he had got in his car and driven the several hours to tell her how he felt and to be with her the week before. The urge to share herself fully with him had become all-consuming.

Paris adjusted the picnic basket she held and giggled to herself as she considered that next time she used the basket perhaps she could find a red cloak to wear. *I wonder how Xavier would feel being the big bad wolf?* The thought made her insides tighten and she considered how she would ask such a question of her well-bred, polite gentleman.

The lift arrived and she waited for a family to exit before getting in and pressing the button for the top floor. Paris continued to hum and fantasize about attacking Xavier when he opened the door, to hell with the food she brought. Now all she hoped was he had not changed from work and he still had his pilot uniform on. It didn't take long for the elevator to arrive at her destination and she checked her appearance in the mirror that was hung in the small alcove that housed the two lifts. Her heavy hair had been curled and then tousled to look like she had just spent an hour getting it to look so artfully natural. Her make-up was a touch of mascara, a hint of lipstick, and enhanced eyebrows. Paris adjusted the straps of her green dress and lifted her breasts a little higher.

Happy for once with what she saw, Paris walked out of the alcove and turned right towards Xavier's apartment, only to find a slender Asian woman leaning against the door frame. She casually swung an overnight bag as she laughed at whatever Xavier had said. Without knowing why, Paris spun back into the alcove, tears sprung up and her chest fought for air. She rapidly hit the down button, trying to remain calm. She would not fall apart here. A sensuous feminine voice traveled down the hall and Paris knew the woman was headed her way. She had no wish to ride in the lift with her. Desperately, Paris looked around and was relieved to spot the emergency exit and quickly opened the door into the stairwell. Her heart pounded as she ran up the stairs to a midpoint landing and no longer able to hold her emotions in a sob escaped her. Dramatically, she slid to the floor.

Thoughts and emotions overwhelmed her as she struggled to understand what she had seen. Images of the woman's bag and her relaxed manner around Xavier made Paris feel ill. Maybe his mother had attempted one final set-up? As she took deep breathes and calmed down, her more sensible side could finally have their say. *You do know that you have done exactly what you promised Xavier you wouldn't do? You jumped to conclusions and assumed the worst because you are scared. He has given you no reason not to trust him.* Paris took several more deep, calming breaths and wiped the tears from her cheeks and chin. *You are going to throw away the man you love more than anything without giving him a chance because some assholes, who are irrelevant, can't see your worth? Are you actually going to let two people who don't matter continue to have control over your happiness?* As she spoke the words to herself she finally came to understand how much power she had given two people who meant nothing to her. The people who loved her, cared for her, and knew her, mattered.

"Stand up and go find out who she was," she spoke aloud. "Get your shit together, Paris. Xavier is yours, now go claim him."

Xavier

A knock at the door made Xavier frown. He was busy trying to get everything ready and the incriminating evidence put away before Paris arrived. He hadn't even managed to have a shower nor get changed. Paris was due to arrive in about fifteen minutes, he hoped whoever it was could be dealt with quickly.

He opened the door to find Paris, holding a picnic basket, standing there. She looked gorgeous in a pretty wrap-around sundress and her hair was shiny and curled. His heart lurched a little when he realized that she had been crying. All thought about hiding evidence and having showers went out the window as all he wanted to do was find out what was wrong with the woman he loved. "Paris, you're early. Is everything okay?" He stepped out of the way to let her in.

"You need to forgive me," she blurted, her eyes sparkling with unshed tears.

Xavier's heart constricted. What had she done that would need forgiveness? He refused to allow his thoughts to jump to the worse scenarios, this was Paris, they were meant to be together, he had to trust in that. "Come, sit and tell me what happened." His voice was calm, yet his emotions were not.

They made it halfway into the lounge kitchen area when she stopped and looked horrified at what she found. "What is all of this?"

He tried not to look guilty. "It's our dinner and breakfast." He looked at the plethora of different-sized Tupperware containers. "I spoke to May a couple of nights ago and told her I wanted to make your night special when I got back, but wouldn't have time to shop. May offered to cook dinner and breakfast for us and Taree's sister just dropped it off."

Paris began to laugh. "I bet there is no dessert in there. Nor anything to drink?"

Xavier frowned. How on earth did she know that? "May said she would take care of both, but I think she forgot."

Paris held out her basket. "She didn't."

What was she talking about? He took the basket from her and put it on the coffee table. Xavier opened it to find champagne and a large, clear container that held chocolate-covered strawberries. Now he understood Paris's laughter. "You spoke to May too?"

"I did. She is the one who suggested drink and dessert."

He sat down on the wide couch and pulled Paris down with him. "Now, tell me what you are sorry about." He gently pushed a curl out of her hazel eyes. Xavier noticed a blush slowly appear on her cheeks.

Paris took his hand and looked at him. She seemed to have calmed down from her original outburst. "I saw Taree's sister leaving and jumped to a few conclusions."

Understanding dawned on him. He let her finish.

"I hid in the stairwell and cried until I realized that I didn't actually know anything, and rather than worry about it or run away I needed to trust you and ask you who she was. I know you love me and I wanted to show you that I loved you too by giving you my complete heart and trust. So I came to apologize and promise I will tell you if I am feeling insecure, and I will not let those high school bastards ruin my future," she finished in a rush.

Xavier sat there, letting her words sink in. "In the middle of that speech did you just say you love me?"

Paris smiled her perfect smile and let go of his hand, she pushed him back into his seat and surprisingly moved to straddle him. Xavier always loved it when she took control. She was beautiful and her curves made him harden within moments of touching her. Paris bent toward him and kissed him softly before moving to his ear. "Yes," she breathed, sending a shiver down his spine and straight to his center. His groin tightened further in response. "I fucking love you."

Xavier laughed, he couldn't help it. It was so Paris to swear while declaring herself. She continued to nibble his ear before moving to his neck and finally his mouth. He reached up and twisted her silky hair around his hand, holding her to him as he deepened the kiss. Xavier's tongue darted in and out, building the heat of their passion. He knew he could spend the remainder of his life doing nothing other than kissing her.

"We need to stop," Paris said as she broke the kiss and sat further back in his lap. His erection begged to differ.

"We really don't." He attempted to pull her back closer to him.

"All the food that May prepared needs to be put away." She arched her eyebrow at him. "Didn't you have something special prepared for this evening? I know I did."

Xavier groaned, unwilling to move. "I did have a special evening planned." He was torn. Paris was right, he needed to put the food away and have a shower, but what he wanted was to devour her, make her his until she called his name, repeatedly telling him that she loved him. The peace he felt at knowing she loved him was intoxicating.

"How about I put the food away and you have a shower?" She leaned forward and bit his bottom lip. "Though I will say that anytime you want to wear that"—she nodded to his uniform-covered chest—"in the bedroom, you just go ahead and do it."

He was shocked and turned on by her words and actions. Life with her would always be entertaining. Paris slid off his lap and helped him to his feet. "Was there anything you wanted me to keep out to eat now?"

"I think we should start with dessert. Strawberries and champagne on the balcony watching the sunset with my girl is a perfect way to start the evening."

The bubbles of champagne-filled her nose and made her giggle as she brought it to her mouth.

"Wait," Xavier said as he filled his glass. "I have something for you before we drink."

Her curiosity peaked. Paris put down the glass and settled into her cushioned chair on the balcony. The early evening summer breeze cooled her skin, and as the sun finally headed for its slumber it cast long shadows across the slowly moving boats that filled her view of the docklands. Xavier cleared his throat, drawing her attention back to him. He put down his champagne flute and pulled out a folded piece of paper from the back pocket of his linen shorts. "I know you don't like resolutions, but I wanted to make you a list of all the things I resolve to do for and with you this year."

A warmth spread throughout her body, that had nothing to do with the hot summer night, as she took in the words of the man who loved her. Rather than her usual eye-rolling, scoffing response, she smiled to let him know she wanted to hear more.

"Once a month we must try a new type of restaurant or food." His smile widened as he watched her.

"Now that is a resolution that works for me." Paris was surprised at the simplicity, yet originality of the idea. Maybe these were things she could get on board with.

"Once a month we must watch something the other one wants us to watch with them."

Paris nodded her agreement as she smirked. They had had quite the debate on what show to watch one night.

"Once a year we will travel to somewhere that is new for both of us."

"And I would like to add that it doesn't need to be overseas. Just somewhere new."

Xavier hesitated over the next one and she watched color rise on his cheeks.

"Once a month I will play one bedroom game of Paris's choosing." He swallowed and shyly looked at her. "I only just added that. Your comment about my uniform gave me the idea."

"That's it?" she asked. "All the resolutions you want to make?"

"Yes, I think from now on resolutions should be fun and aimed at being together."

Paris took her glass and held it up to Xavier. "It's a great idea but it is no longer New Year's Eve."

"No, but it is Chinese New Year and we do have champagne, so close enough."

She holds up her glass. "To champagne resolutions."

As she took a sip of the heavenly liquid, Paris came to a

quick decision. She had planned for it after dinner but now seemed a perfect time. Screwing up her courage she stood and quickly closed the gap between them. With her free hand she took hold of the front of his shirt and pulled him toward her, "Kiss me," she demanded.

Xavier put his arm around her waist and drew her to him. She melted into him as his lips came down on hers and instantly widened to seek out her tongue. Paris slid her tongue along his in a slow intimate pattern and she pushed her hips against him, feeling his hard cock already straining to escape. They broke apart and she let go of his shirtfront to slide her hand down his sculptured chest and over the mound of his pants. She watched him close his eyes with pleasure and she felt her need for him grow.

"Grab the bottle," she told him as she took the plate filled with chocolate-covered strawberries. "Hope you don't mind food in your bedroom," she said over her shoulder as she walked into the lounge and headed for the master bedroom. Once there, she put her glass and plate on the bedside table, then went to take his glass and the bottle.

Xavier moved to close the heavy curtain against the sunlight that lingered due to daylight savings. "No, leave it open," Paris spoke, her words didn't waver.

He looked surprised but not unhappy. "Are you sure?"

Paris took hold of her final fears and looked at the man who worshiped her and whom she loved more than breathing. It was time to take that final step in freeing herself of her insecurities created so long ago by people who meant nothing to her, and replace them with truth and self-love. "I don't think you want to miss out on this." Slowly she untied the knot on her wrap-around dress and let it slide off her shoulders. She was astounded at how sexy and completely unselfconscious she felt.

Paris was wearing the black and red tulle and taffeta come-fuck-me dress that she had bought from Shirl all those years ago. By the way Xavier's tongue ran along his lips and his eyes widened in appreciation, she knew he was pleased. "You are in so much trouble," he drew the words out into a sensuous sentence that made her insides clench.

She let the dress fall to the floor and casually picked up the glass and drained it before holding it out for him to refill. Paris had never felt so desirable as she did at that moment. "What sort of trouble did you have in mind?"

If you enjoyed the book please consider leaving a review on your favourite place to purchase and/or Goodreads and/or Bookbub.

This helps the author immensely.

Don't forget if you want to receive information, news and exclusive offers please sign up for the

Taya Rune Newsletter:

https://www.tayarune.com/subscribe

ACKNOWLEDGMENTS

I would like to take a few moments to say thank you to the
people who have supported me along this journey.

To my husband, thank you for being my partner in crime.
I love the way you still make me laugh.

To my children, thank you for teaching me to let go of the
small stuff.
I am proud of you.

To my family, thank you for the love and support you have
shown me throughout the years.

To my friends, the ones that have my back and are forever in
my corner
I cherish you.

To my editor, Rochelle J. Simas –
IDK art.

Thank you for the kind words that always accompany the return of my fabulously edited manuscripts.

To my PA – Book Queen.
Thanx for doing so much of the behind the scenes heavy lifting for me.
I am forever grateful for you.

To my ARC, Street and Beta Teams.
You rock!

To my cover designer - LC Taylor Publishings.
My contemporary covers look amazing thanks to you.

To my formatter - BBB Publishings.
Thank you for always squeezing me in and making my books look professional.

And to my readers, thank you for your continued support, it means the world to me. Xox

ABOUT TAYA RUNE

Taya Rune is a writer of romance, a sucker for happy endings and has a knack for asking people uncomfortable questions.

She is a member of the Romance Writer's of Australia and has had her work published in different anthologies and publications.

Taya resides in Melbourne and loves the unpredictable weather, the varied cultures, food, and great stage shows, and that there is always something new to experience.

www.ingramcontent.com/pod-product-compliance
Lightning Source LLC
Chambersburg PA
CBHW030803190726
48285CB00003B/998